A SHORT & SWEET CHRISTMAS ROMANCE COLLECTION

VOLUME 1

ANNE HARRISON

CONTENTS

KATE AND THE CHRISTMAS RIDE

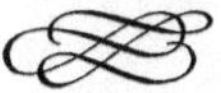

PAXTON JONES, DRIVER

Expensive heels clicked on the linoleum outside Kate Chesterton's office door. That could only mean that her boss Maureen LaCroix was coming. Sitting at her desk, Kate fit her thumbs under her collar, smoothing out the neckline of her light blue power suit. Happily, she had just had this outfit starched at the dry cleaner. One flip of her hair and she was ready for the boss to come in. Maureen didn't knock.

"Kate, do you have those mock-ups ready?"

Kate shuffled through the organized piles of papers on her desk. "Of course. Here it is." She slid the laminated artwork out from underneath the other options and handed it to her. Despite the inconvenience of hard copies, Kate preferred them, and she suspected that they set her apart from some of the others at the marketing firm. At least, she hoped so. "This one's for the billboard."

Maureen's lacquered fingernail clicked against the cardboard as she took the mock-up from her. "This looks pretty good. I think Wetta will approve." A half-smile snuck onto her face.

That was a good sign. Kate sat up straighter in her

ergonomically supportive office chair. Why did she always have to slump?

"Send me the files," Maureen said, her slight southern accent shone through her words. Maybe that was why the clients thought she was more relatable and less of a shark. "You have the other versions of this concept?"

"They should already be in your inbox." Kate smiled.

Maureen nodded. "Great. I'll get back to you when I see them. Good work."

One day, Kate could barge into other people's offices and demand to see their work. She would organize the ad campaigns and make them more cohesive and arresting than most of the holiday-themed drivel she'd seen in magazines and L-train terminals the past few weeks.

Twisting around on the ball of her foot, Maureen left, black pencil skirt hugging her hips as she walked out of the office and closed the door behind her.

Kate checked her hair again in the dark window behind her desk. Nothing out of place. *Good work.* Did that mean that she would be promoted soon? Normally, Maureen only gave her critiques, never unqualified praise. That *must* mean a promotion soon.

And then she could actually afford the apartment where she lived by herself above the Loop. She knew she should probably live farther away from the office, but she wanted to be right where the action was, even if the cost of living was five times what she had known growing up in Ohio.

A year ago, she had even sold her car to keep up with the rent. She didn't need it anyway. She never went back home, and Chicago had a good network of public transportation. Who needed to rub shoulders with Chicago drivers? They had certainly scared her half to death when she'd gotten here three years ago.

She double-checked her inbox. Yes, she had sent the other graphics.

One glance at the clock told her that normal working hours were ending. Most of the employees at TKL Solutions were packing up their bags and heading home.

She wouldn't stay much longer. Maybe just a couple…

"Hey there! Heading out?" The perky voice belonged to her friend Lucy who swung in at the door like Kramer from *Seinfeld*. She was petite, blonde, and not too full of herself. A good combination.

"Mm maybe." From the moment Kate was hired, she had been drawn to Lucy. Together, they had gone out a couple times for drinks. Most weekends were for catching up on extra work, but Kate tried to squeeze in a happy hour here and there.

Lucy's blonde curls bobbed at her shoulders as she cocked her head. "You're not staying longer, are you?"

"I really need to finish up a couple things."

Lucy huffed. "You always say that, and it isn't true. You know what you need?"

Kate crossed her arms over her blazer.

"You need to relax. Come on! Let's go to Joey's." Lucy drew a small tube of lipstick from the purse slung over her arm, uncapped it, drew the red end over her lips, and popped it back in her purse. "It'll be fun. What other twenty-three-year-old just works all the time without going out, letting loose…?"

"The 30 under 30 list, that's who!" But she was starting to warm up to the idea. Maybe the Christmas lights on the street were starting to get to her. Merry times and all that.

"Girl, I'm taking you out whether you want to go or not! Grab your stuff." Lucy switched her purse to the other shoulder.

Kate wasn't sure she wanted to go out. It's not like she would pick up a man in a power suit. Every website and magazine told her it wasn't feminine enough. But then, she didn't have time for a relationship right now, anyway. She could barely make time for her friend.

She rolled her eyes. "Fine!" she groaned, pointing at Lucy. "But I'll just stay late on Monday."

Now it was Lucy's turn to roll her eyes. "I know you will. That's why you need to unwind tonight."

Kate turned off her computer (almost getting caught up in answering more emails until Lucy eyed her with that knowing look), grabbed her purse, and headed out. The two of them walked at a clip down the hallway.

Rounding the corner, they almost ran into Fred, the old janitor. He had worked there since long before Kate was hired, and he always had a smile for everybody. More and more paraphernalia hung off his cleaning cart by the year—little stuffed animals, flags from different countries, colored ribbons. This time of year, he added candy canes and snowman ornaments.

"Good night, Fred!" Kate sang as she passed him.

"Leaving so soon?" he asked. "Isn't it just five o' clock?"

"I'm going out," she announced.

He chuckled. "Good job, Lucy. I don't think that many people could get this one to leave the office."

A twist of guilt tugged at Kate's stomach. Should she stay instead of going out for drinks?

As though she could read her thoughts, Lucy grabbed her arm and gave it a little squeeze. "I'm taking her, and she won't be coming back until Monday!"

Fred shook his head. When they didn't move, he said, "Well, go on, then!"

"Aye, aye," said Lucy, and they both hurried off to the elevator.

*T*inny Mariah Carey songs played above the din at the bar. A mix of neon and yellow artisan lights cast deep shadows on the sea of faces. Kate and Lucy nestled up to the bar. Lucy kept spinning her barstool around. Probably to make sure the men there knew she was available. Kate kept her stool angled at Lucy as she slowly stirred her second Long Island with the double straw.

"Oh, what about that one?" Lucy lowered her head and pointed across the bar to a man with a blond beard who saw exactly what she was doing.

Kate hunched further over her drink, not sure if the warmth she felt on her face was the flush of alcohol or embarrassment. "Please, I said I'd go out with you, not that I'd pick up strange men."

"He doesn't seem strange," she said, giving the guy a little wave.

"You literally know nothing about him! He could be an ax murderer!"

"Why does everyone say that?" Lucy spun her chair back around. "Are there that many ax murderers? Isn't a normal murderer bad enough?"

"Maybe everybody just read *Crime and Punishment* in high school," Kate muttered.

Her point still stood. That guy could live at home and breed shih tzus. He could eat blocks of bleu cheese like apples. They didn't know.

"Well, I think he's nice," Lucy said.

Kate took another sip of her Long Island. The situation was slowly getting funnier. She giggled, struck by inspiration. "We can take a bet! I bet he's a weirdo and you think he's great. Go up and talk to him for five minutes. If I'm right, you buy my drink." She did a quick calculation in her head to figure out how much time at the office that would equate to. More than five minutes.

"You're on!" Lucy hopped from her seat and bee-lined to the guy with the beard. His eyes widened as he saw her walking with such purpose. He shifted almost nervously in his seat.

Hopefully he wasn't too terrible. Kate didn't want a creeper following them home. Still, she was sure she just won a free drink.

Lucy tossed her hair sweetly over one shoulder as she reached him. He gave her a big smile, but Kate couldn't hear anything they were saying.

The couple next to her at the bar were talking about their respective families' Christmas traditions. Their voices were too smooth and smiles too ready. First date.

The guys at the end of the bar talked about their shifts in the factory, peppering their conversation with profanity and bursts of course laughter.

A bodacious woman in a pink dress leaned against the bar, nearly pressing up against her, to order a Mistletoe Martini.

Kate pursed her lips and took another sip of her drink. Her eyes drifted over the bottle labels and neon signs behind the bar. Some of the bottles were hard to read, but the color or design would give the idea the company wanted to portray—fun and flirty, laid back and tropical, dark and sexy. For a lot of these companies, it wasn't about the name. It was about the experience. People remembered experiences.

A glass clinked in front of her. Another Long Island.

"I didn't…" she began.

The barkeeper gestured with a tattooed hand. "Courtesy of the gentlemen over there."

She spun around. Blond beard guy. He and Lucy were watching for her reaction. She smiled despite herself, huffing out a sigh. Three for the price of two. Sly girl.

Lucy danced to her feet and hurried back to her stool. She didn't sit down. "See," she said, "I told you!"

Kate slurped down the rest of Long Island #2 and switched glasses with the full one. "You were right. This time."

Lucy bent a little closer so the first date couple couldn't hear. "His name is Mark and we're getting along really well." Excitement and smiles proved her words.

Kate felt an odd sense of loss. "Then go back over there. He sounds great."

"Oh, I don't know. I don't want to leave you all alone." But her eyes were pleading for permission.

"It's fine. I'm great right here." She fished her phone out of her purse with one hand as she spoke.

"You sure?"

"Of course! Go, go!" She plunked the phone on the slightly sticky wooden bar top. She could knock out some emails while she was gone.

Lucy beamed. "Okay! I won't be gone too long."

Kate opened her inbox. Eighty-two messages. She could answer those now so they wouldn't pile up on Monday morning.

The subject line of one message, from Maureen, read "Important - Wetta Account."

"Santa Baby" by Eartha Kitt seeped into her consciousness. She hated that song. Why did they have to play it every Christmas? What kind of a person—?

Focus. She had to focus. The little words on the screen were swimming as though she had watery eyes. What was important about that account?

Maureen had never been one to mince words. "Acme wants to add another email list campaign, social media personality, and TV commercial all connected with brand new content. If you can pull this off to their satisfaction before the new year, you have the promotion."

Kate blinked. Did that say "you have the promotion"? She blinked again to be sure. No, not yet.

If she nailed this new campaign, *then* she would have the

promotion. That would mean no more second-hand couches for her apartment and would set her up for long-term career success.

She bit her lip and then bit the little black double straw. Those long nights were about to pay off. Sure, there would be more long nights ahead, but this was what she lived for—the rush, the deadlines, the happy customers, the rising sales numbers. She had a knack for these things.

Spinning her stool around, she found Lucy and Mark locked in deep conversation. Their hands both sat on the table, nearly touching. Any minute now.

Maybe she should go back to the office. Gripping the cold glass a little tighter, she remembered that she had promised her friend she wouldn't work anymore this weekend.

Besides, she was definitely starting to feel a buzz. She gulped down the last of the Long Island.

The festive atmosphere circled around her but didn't touch her, and suddenly she wanted to go home. Lucy could stay as long as she wanted with Mark, but she wanted to be away from all these people.

She waved down the bartender to pay, pushed herself up from the chair, thankful for the flats she had changed into on the train. Heels would only have made walking more complicated. The hardwood floor had sneaky edges.

In a second, she was at the table where the lovebirds sat. "I'm going home," she told Lucy, and then wheeled on the guy. "It's lovely meeting you, Mark."

He looked a little surprised. He had introduced himself, right?

Lucy knit her brows and let go of Mark's right hand to lay it gently on Kate's arm. "It's getting really cold out there."

"I have a jacket."

"I think you should call an Über."

Mark nodded. "That wind is killer."

"That's why they call it the Windy City," Kate said. "It's windy." But they seemed to have gotten the joke the first time.

"Yeah." Lucy got out her phone. "I'll just call you an Über and they'll come and take you home."

"I always take the train."

"I know. And I don't care. I want you to be safe."

"I'm safe."

"Yes." Lucy pressed the last button with a flourish. "Now you are. He'll be here in less than five minutes right outside." She smiled triumphantly and twined her fingers with Mark's as soon as they were free. He rubbed the back of her hands with his thumbs as if they were already together.

How could she protest? It wasn't that big of a deal, and Lucy offered to pay again. She had to remember so she could pick up the tab next time. In her mind, she shuffled budget categories so there would be a little extra to use when the time came.

"Fine. You win." She moved away from the new couple to the front door where freezing wind kept seeping through the opening any time someone opened it. Which was often.

Kate wrapped her jacket more closely around herself. Maybe Lucy was right after all. Kate had lived in Chicago long enough to know that even walking to Ogilvy was murder if an ice storm was coming. Her first winter here had chapped her raw. For a couple days at work, she looked like she had a skin disease.

An Über sticker peeked out the windshield of a dark blue Subaru Forester. Was that him? She held her breath and rushed out the glass doors into the cold. She pointed at the man behind the wheel and he responded by leaning over and opening the passenger door.

Was he new? Über was supposed to work like a taxi. The driver drove and the passenger sat in the back. She opened the door to the back seat and slid in behind the driver.

At an unnatural sideways angle, he slammed the passenger door shut. Then he gripped the seat and twisted around to smile at her. He was only a couple years older than she was. Dark wavy hair, five o' clock shadow, dimpled smile, blue eyes. Not half bad.

"Hey, my name's Paxton," he said in a warm baritone. "Where are you going today?"

She gave him her address.

He faced the front and plugged the address into his GPS. "Oh, that's a nice part of town. You must be some kind of high-powered lawyer or something. Am I right?"

"Not exactly." But she was more than an Über driver.

They pulled away from the bar into the terrifying Friday night Chicago traffic.

"Did you see *Hamilton?*"

"What?"

"The musical, *Hamilton.*"

"A few months ago, why?"

"Did you like it?"

"Sure." She took out her phone again. She could answer a couple more emails and send the signal to this guy that she didn't feel like making small talk.

"As a kid in the Caribbean I wished for a war." He started singing, rapping.

"What the!" The words sounded a little familiar, but what was he doing? Who wanted a rapping driver?

"That's from the opening of *Hamilton.* I thought you knew."

She did know. Now that he reminded her. "Well, yeah, but you don't need to do a one-man show."

"Okay." He held up the one hand she could see in mock surrender. "I just try to make every ride special, you know? If people remember you, they might come back." He dug in his pocket and handed her a warm business card: *Paxton Jones, driver.* His number was on the back. "You can always call me directly if you want a ride. The app sends the request out to everyone, and it's every man for himself."

"Or woman."

"Or woman, right. So how can I make the ride special for you?"

"Just silence is fine," she said, staring down at her phone.

"Okay. As long as you're sure. There are snacks in the center console if you want them." He gently patted it beside him with a calloused hand.

"Thanks, Patrick."

"Paxton. Or Pax. Pax is fine too. You never told me your name."

"Kate."

"Oh, that's nice." He tried it out. "Kate."

Lights ran by in blurs and after images. Steel structures plunged the car into shadow over and over again as they drove beneath overpasses.

In a couple minutes, her apartment building came into view. She bent down to see the eighteenth floor through the car window.

"You're way up there?" Paxton eyed her through the side mirror. He leaned his forearm against the cold window.

"Just pull up there," she said, pointing to the curb.

He did as she asked. She wavered just a little getting out of the car. Her flat caught on the crack between the curb and the sidewalk.

"Have a good night!" he waved and pulled away, leaving her alone on the windy street.

HOME FOR CHRISTMAS

Sitting at the staff lunch table, Kate stuffed a forkful of salad into her mouth. She had been there since six, and her shoulders were getting stiff from sitting at her desk all morning.

Lucy glided in with the glazed eyes of a woman who was definitely twitterpated. Kate smiled as Lucy sat next to her. "Oh my goodness!" Lucy cried in a voice just low enough that the whole room couldn't hear. "Oh my goodness! Mark and I talked all night. I think they had to kick us out of that bar."

"Thanks for paying for the ride," Kate chimed in.

Lucy waved her hand. "It was nothing. I'm telling you." She hummed. "Mmm hm. This might be the one."

Kate raised an eyebrow. "The one? Really? The guy from the bar?"

"Yes!" She looked scandalized. "Did you see him?"

"He did get me a drink. He was pretty nice."

"Oh, he was more than nice." Lucy lowered her lids suggestively.

"Okay," Kate said, changing the subject, "I'm glad, but did you make any more progress on the Wetta account?"

"Not over the weekend. We're not all like you!" Lucy hit her lightly on the shoulder. She just meant to tease, but there was an edge that Kate didn't like.

She stabbed a lettuce leaf.

But Lucy would not be dissuaded. "Hey, are you coming to our Christmas party?"

"I'm not sure." Christmas wasn't her favorite holiday. The ice prevented her from staying at work as late as she could during other times of the year. Bing Crosby was nice, and something warm blossomed in her chest when she heard him sing "White Christmas" but still...

Her cell phone rang.

"Oh, I have to get that!" Kate nearly flew out of her chair to answer the call. "Hello, this is Kate Chesterton."

"Kate, do you always give your first and last name?" said an amused voice Kate would know anywhere.

"Mom?"

"Hey, sweetie! I feel like I haven't talked to you in so long!"

"You know I'm at work, right? Maybe you can call back a little later."

"No, no. I called about something important."

Kate's stomach filled with ice. "Is... everything okay?"

"Oh yes, yes. I just wanted to know if you're coming home for Christmas this year. We haven't heard from you."

"I wasn't planning on it." She held up her hand to hide her mouth from the rest of staff taking lunch. "Mom, I'm all set for a promotion. If I can just nail this..."

"Your brother's getting married."

Kate's mouth fell open. Did she even know he had a girlfriend? "Brian's getting married? To whom?"

"Her name is Jessica. She's very nice. You need to meet her before he proposes." Mom lowered her voice. "Kate, he wants you to be there when he proposes on Christmas Eve."

Kate felt like ropes were being tied around her body, like she couldn't move. She couldn't go home now, not when this job was so close! But she couldn't deny a once-in-a-lifetime request like this either. Immediately the December calendar flashed through her mind. Maybe she could work until the twenty-third and then…

"Kate?"

"Yes?"

"Will you come? Brian will be devastated if you don't. And the rest of us haven't seen you in such a long time."

A pause. "Okay. I'll be there. I just can't stay very long, Mom."

"Ooh!" Her voice went up with glee. "Wonderful! When can we expect you?"

"Christmas Eve."

"You have to come out before that. Jessica is staying the entire week."

"Well, she doesn't have a possible promotion at one of the biggest ad agencies in Chicago."

"Kate!"

"Fine. I'll come on the twenty-third."

The pause on the other end of the line meant a contented sigh. "I'm so glad we'll get to see you again, sweetie. Chicago isn't that far away but you never drive down."

Six hours. She'd say that was pretty far. "I don't have a car any more, remember?"

Mom gasped. "Why not?"

"I don't need one."

"Then how will you come down for Christmas?"

That was a good question. Train? They didn't go so far… "I'll figure it out," she said. Why did her parents have to live in such a tiny, backwater town?

A note of uncertainty rang in Mom's voice. "Okay. Just let us know if you need anything."

I need to be able to do my work this Christmas instead of spending twelve hours in the car. "All right, Mom."

"Love you."

"Love you too." Click.

Lucy sauntered over, seeing that the call had ended. "What was that all about? You don't seem very happy."

"My brother's getting married."

Lucy beamed. "Oh, that's a good thing! …Right?"

"Yeah, that part's good, but now I have to go home for Christmas."

Lucy raised an eyebrow.

"I have to meet the fiancée. He's going to propose on Christmas Eve."

Lucy gasped. "Oh Kate! That's so romantic!"

"I guess so." Hearing "Feliz Navidad" on the radio for the millionth time didn't exactly set the mood for her, but her brother was different.

"You know, I'm glad you have to go home. Honestly, I worry about you sometimes."

"There's nothing to worry about." Kate made her way back to her salad. "I like working. Nobody seems to get that part. And I'm good at it!"

"You're very good at it," Lucy confirmed. "But I'm still glad that you're forced to spend the holidays with your family instead of here with Maureen and Fred!"

"Okay, fine. You win. The universe wins! I'm going home for Christmas."

The next few days passed in a blur. Kate stayed late every day, trying in vain to catch up with everything she had to do to earn the promotion. Lucy circled around her, giving updates on her budding relationship with Blond Beard Mark. Maureen kept dangling incentives (and extra work) in front of her face.

Before she knew it, December twenty-second had come, and Kate still had no idea how she was getting home to southeastern Ohio. If she took an Über, she could continue to work in the back seat while the driver chauffeured her. Some uninterrupted time—she could use that right now. It seemed like everyone wanted something from her at the office.

Kate pulled out her phone and pushed back her office chair from her desk. She would just book a ride.

The view from the windows was like glitter swirling in black water. Dim honking sounded below.

After a couple tries, she figured there were only two possibilities: there was a glitch in the app, or Moscow, Ohio, was out of Über's radius.

She cursed under her breath. She hadn't expected that. She *should* have expected it, but she had been so focused on this ad campaign that she hadn't spared a thought for transportation. And she had to leave first thing in the morning. Very first thing. She would pack a few things as soon as she got home and set an alarm for 4:00 A.M. kind of early. She'd promised.

She fought the urge to pick at her perfectly painted pink nails. Shoving the phone back in her purse, her finger caught on a small piece of stiff paper. She grabbed the card and pulled it out: *Paxton Jones, driver.*

He did say he wanted more jobs. Driving six hours from Chicago to Moscow would earn him plenty of money, and would give her the freedom to work six hours, effectively making back anything she spent on the trip. She twirled the card between her fingers a few times before digging around for her phone again. He was her only option.

Ring, ring… "Hey, this is Paxton." His deep voice sounded a little too casual.

"Hello, this is Kate Chesterton, from the other day. I'm going to need a ride tomorrow. I was wondering how far you drive."

"That all depends. Where do you want to go?"

"I need to go to Moscow, Ohio, as soon as possible."

There was silence on the other end. He was probably calculating the distance. Suddenly, he laughed. "I can see your problem!" he cried. "That's pretty far, but I'm actually headed the same way. I'll still need to charge the normal rate..."

"That's fine."

"This is great. You're in luck! When should I pick you up tomorrow?"

Kate pulled her fingers away from her nail. "Um, when's the earliest you can come?"

"The earliest? I can come any time, ma'am."

"Four thirty?"

"Four thirty it is. I'll just pull up to the valet."

"You remember where I live?"

"It was only a couple days ago. Remember, I always try to make each experience special." She could hear his dimpled smile in his tone.

Hopefully she hadn't made a bad decision. She was trusting this stranger to get her home safely, but she knew nothing about him. Maybe he was a creeper who had memorized her address to stalk her...

"All right, have a good night, ma'am. I'll pick you up in the morning."

She swallowed. "Okay, you too."

JOHN LENNON

The next morning, Kate was too bleary eyed to care if Paxton were an ax murderer or not. She'd dressed down. Rarely was she able to do that nowadays. With so much time at the office, she had practically lived in power suits. Today she wore her biggest jeans and an oversized white sweater.

She rolled her black, carry-on-sized suitcase across the frigid concrete to the Forester. Icy wind whipped across the front of her apartment complex. Glad she had brought her puffy purple coat, she propped the suitcase upright at the back of the car.

Paxton hopped out, opened the trunk, and shoved it in. He didn't look tired enough. Well, that was probably a good thing. One of them needed to be conscious for this drive.

She wearily got herself into the back seat and glanced at the watch she had given herself last Christmas. She would take ten minutes to relax. Just ten. And then she'd get to work as she had promised herself.

Paxton got back into the warm car, rubbing his hands together. Cold air followed him and radiated off the back of his coat for a moment. "Good morning!" he said.

She fought the urge to groan. Too perky. She made a sound that she hoped he would take as a response.

"All right, let's go!"

They pulled away from the curb and merged back into Chicago traffic. Because of course there was traffic at this time of night—or was it morning?

"Hey, you still want silence?"

"Mm hm."

As they passed Millennium Park and saw the white lights shimmering in all the trees, it clicked. Holiday traffic. She had planned to be back midday. This traffic had better not mess up her plans.

She laid her head back on the cloth seat. She hadn't even done her hair today. It felt soft and tangly, but she didn't care. Opening one eye, she held her wrist up to her face. Nine minutes had gone by. How was that possible? They had just left!

She stretched her hands in front of her and gave a huge yawn. Scraping the inside of her eye with a painted fingernail, she got out her phone again. There was no time to waste if this ride was going to be worth it.

She answered emails and made calls and approved ad copy until the city was behind them and the sun was above. And they were creeping behind miles of stop-and-go cars.

"Could we get off at the next exit and pass some of these people?" she finally asked, shifting in her seat. Pulling forward, easing to another stop, rolling further, rushing a few feet, halting —it was all giving her claustrophobia. And nausea.

Paxton pointed at his smartphone screen mounted over the dashboard. "That wouldn't make any difference. See that red line? There's traffic for a few miles before it breaks up."

"Ugh!" When she looked down at her screen again, gorge rose a few centimeters up in her throat. She quickly looked away. Did she have any Dramamine?

Forward. Stop. Forward. Stop.

"Is there a gas station near here?"

"We just passed the last one for a while. Why? Do you need to stop?" Paxton looked at her through the rearview mirror.

With each response, she felt sicker than before. For a moment she didn't answer.

"You okay?"

"I'm fine." Her breath hitched. She revised. "Yes, I need to stop." What had Mom taught her? Breathe in, steady breaths, look at something that isn't moving.

His face turned apologetic in the mirror. "I'll pull off as soon as I can, but that won't be for a few minutes."

"Do you have Dramamine?"

"Car sick? Just jump up front. That always helps." He patted the passenger seat. "I'm not surprised. You were looking at your phone since we left. Here, just hop out as soon as I stop again." The white truck's brake lights already shone red ten feet ahead of them.

His idea was better than nothing. She had to get her rising nausea under control before she could focus on anything else.

They rocked to a stop. She flung the door open and he leaned over to open the side door for her, just as he had the other night. Billowing cold surrounded her as she swept around the back of the car. Jumping back inside, she slammed the door. They rolled forward a few more feet.

"There you go!" he said, smiling at her. He had stripped off his big coat and wore a red plaid flannel underneath. Only his left hand gripped the wheel. They weren't exactly in a high-speed chase, so it didn't matter.

She wasn't feeling a lot better, but her stomach started to settle enough to tell her this was the right decision.

"So you're from Ohio?" he began.

She side-eyed him.

"You need a distraction. You're from Ohio?"

"Yes."

"But now you live in a very nice place in Chicago."

"Mm hm."

"How did that happen?"

She didn't feel like the relating the whole story. "Just wanted to get out of there," she said vaguely.

"Oh, come on! You know that's not how you got there. But fine, if you don't want to talk, I can talk."

Of course he could.

He rubbed one strong hand over the stubble on his jaw as though he were thinking of which entertaining story to tell.

"Mm," he hummed, a low rumble. "I used to live in Ohio too. Just moved away last year." Deep eyes flashed in her direction. "It's hard to make a living in a little town, even if you love it, you know?"

She took a deep, slow breath. His story wasn't helping her stomach.

He continued without her acknowledgement. "Chicago, on the other hand, is full of people, so I thought I'd come out and see what I could do here."

"You have family?" she asked reluctantly. Lame distraction was better than no distraction.

"Parents and sisters live back in Ohio." He pointed ahead.

She glanced at his hand on the wheel. No ring. So that was it for family, then.

"One sister is close to my age, and then there are two younger ones. They all chose to stay. One of these days I'll probably go back too."

"Why would you want to live in a tiny little town when you could be somewhere else?"

"Chicago's not exactly family-oriented. Everybody's out for themselves. I like the slower pace. The coffee guy still knows my name back home. You just don't get that in a big city."

Visions of *Seinfeld* and *Friends* flashed across her mind. Didn't the servers in the New York coffee shops know those characters?

They seemed to go to cafés more than they went to their jobs. No one needed a small town for that. Kate hadn't personally noticed that level of service in Chicago, but she probably could develop rapport with waiters if she went out more.

His down-home attitude was quaint, but a little nauseating —not what she needed right now. She stretched her back and tried to focus on the white Ford truck.

Paxton let out a little breath. Maybe he could sense her impatience with his story. "Okay," he said, as an elementary school teacher would if he were changing subjects. "You get to meet a famous person—any person, alive or dead. Who do you choose?"

"I don't know."

"Think about it."

Centering herself by staring at the scuff on the right side of the Ford's bumper, she considered. "John Lennon."

"Why?"

When she was small, her dad would play Beatles CD's in the house and she would do those awkward, hip-shaking toddler dances to the music. Dad had laughed with her and swept her up in his arms. She still listened to those songs when she was sad. "I like his music," she said.

"Yeah, it's pretty good."

She whirled on him. "Pretty good? It's great!"

"Right, it's not bad." His dimple showed on his cheek. He knew he was irking her.

"You just don't appreciate good music." She crossed her arms.

He raised his eyebrows. "Excuse me. Did you hear me the other night? I was prepared to give you a one-man show of *Hamilton.*"

"That's not singing."

His eyes popped with exaggerated horror and he flexed his hand on the steering wheel as though he could turn it inside out. He looked a lot stronger than the average driver, who tended to grow flabby over time. "You have no taste, so I have to forgive you."

She resisted the urge to smack him. He gave a half-smile when he saw her hand twitch. "Who would you meet?" she asked defiantly.

"Bernini."

"She sounds pretty."

"No, he was a sculptor. *Apollo and Daphne?*"

She shook her head. She didn't know anything about sculpture, unless she counted *The David*. And there was one with a guy thinking, his head resting on his fist. But she didn't know the name of that sculptor either.

He blew out a breath, as though just the thought of the piece impressed him. "Her hands are turning into leaves and tree branches. It's just… crazy how somebody could make that out of marble. It's so detailed. And the looks on their faces. He has one piece that's just a head." He drew his hand horizontally across his collarbone. "And the guy looks like he's screaming. Maybe he's mad or surprised. I'm telling you, he's good."

"What's his name again?"

"Bernini."

Paxton didn't look high class, with his scruff and plaid, but apparently he appreciated that stuff. She blinked and realized that she didn't feel sick to her stomach anymore.

THE STORM

Well, Paxton wasn't that high class, Kate thought as he chewed a Slim Jim at the gas station. Clouds had come over and looked dark and threatening, even though it was only 10:30. This didn't look good. The weather had put her in a bad mood. She was supposed to be home by now, but they were still an hour and a half away, and that was in good weather with no traffic.

He plunked a coffee cup in front of her. She pulled it over and took a sip. Scorching bitterness coated her tongue like toxic sludge. "Oh my gosh, that's disgusting!" she cried. She slammed the coffee back on the plastic tabletop and slid it away from her. Now she wouldn't be able to taste Christmas dinner. Her taste buds felt rough against the roof of her mouth.

"What? You only drink Starbucks?" he asked, easing into the seat next to her at the little table.

"No, but seriously—that was gross!" She made a face to punctuate her statement. A high whistle drew her eyes to the big windows. The snow came faster now, blowing white across the storefront. She shivered to look at it.

"You guys had better head out now if you don't want to get stuck in this storm."

Kate turned to find the owner of the accented voice that whistled the *s*'s. The man at the table next to them wore a beat-up baseball cap, thick mustache, and Carhartt jacket. He had a cup of that nasty stuff that passed for coffee and peered out the window like a seasoned sailor checking the wind. Probably a trucker. She turned away, hoping he was just crazy.

Paxton spoke up, leaning forward with his forearms on the table. "Is it supposed to get worse?" Concern darkened his handsome features.

The man blew on his mustache. "Oh yeah. If you don't want to stay here tonight, you'd better go." A fresh gust of white rattled the front window. "See what I'm sayin'?"

Paxton turned to Kate. "I don't think we can get to Moscow today, then…"

"Let me just check." She looked up the weather on her phone. *Wow.* That was quite a storm. And it had come out of nowhere. "Oh no!" she groaned. "Then what can we do? I have to get back for Christmas Eve; otherwise, this whole trip is worthless!" The florescent lights started to give her a headache. No wonder she didn't love Christmas. This was a nightmare.

"I'll get you there," he soothed. "Don't worry. But we have to think about tonight."

"I am worried!" She flung her white-sweatered arms in the air and plopped them back on the table. "We can definitely get back by tonight. It's not even noon. I'm not staying anywhere with you."

His eyebrows twitched down. "I'm not doing this for kicks. I think it might be really dangerous out there."

"We'll just see. Let's go. Maybe if we go now, we can beat it." She stood, grabbing her puffy coat and purse. She left the coffee.

Paxton took a contemplative bite of Slim Jim. "Okay. I think I know where we can go."

wo hours later, it was clear that they weren't getting to Moscow. The roads had become so white and slippery that no one could see the lanes. Cars just crept forward with their lights on, hoping their tires would find some tread. Sky was as dark as evening.

Kate popped another Dramamine she had picked up at the gas station. She still sat up front, just in case. The ice made her so nervous that she couldn't focus on doing her work, which just made her more anxious.

Her mom was sad when she heard she couldn't make it until Christmas Eve, but Kate promised her that she would be there —one way or another, so help her!—in time for Brian's proposal.

Night was still a long way off, so she hadn't said a word to Paxton about his plan for tonight, if he had one. The whole situation knotted her stomach. The trip was never supposed to go this way. If they had to stop at a hotel, she was getting separate rooms. No need for this to turn into a Lifetime movie. But she hoped it wouldn't come to that. After paying for this drive, she would hardly be able to afford it.

Slowly, cautiously, Paxton started to turn the wheel, the veins standing out in his hands from gripping so hard. The exit didn't look familiar. "Where are you going?" she asked.

"This is my exit. My family's down here." He stared straight ahead. "I'm going to head to my parents' house. It's pretty big. If the storm stays like this, I'm sure they'll let us stay overnight."

"Hang on! Hang on a second! Your parents' house?" She grimaced at him.

"We don't have a lot of options," he said grimly. In a moment, he brightened. "I was going to see them over the holidays anyway. I just wasn't planning to bring… you."

"Yeah, this wasn't in my plan either." She racked her brain for an alternative. There had to be something. But nothing came to mind. Why stay in an expensive hotel if they could stay somewhere for free? And there would be other people around, so she wouldn't be alone with a stranger. She hated to admit that it wasn't the worst idea. It was *almost* the worst. With the storm, they couldn't do anything about it.

His parents didn't live far off the freeway. The world was a block of blowing gray snow, so she couldn't see the town at all. She could barely make out the house when they rolled onto the driveway. White colonial. Typical Ohio.

Something inside her relaxed when they came to a stop. The location didn't make her happy, but at least he wouldn't kill them both in a fiery crash. They stretched their arms back into their coats and braced themselves before opening the doors.

"Grab your stuff, grab your stuff!" he said with the urgency of a quarterback trying to beat the clock. He opened the hatch and tossed her the bag. Too cold to complain, she scurried after him up the steps to the porch.

Paxton opened the metal flap of the attached mailbox and stuck his hand inside. The house key. She danced on the balls of her feet as he unlocked the door. They both practically fell inside.

Gingerbready warmth enveloped her like a bath. She took a deep breath and surveyed the entry of the house. Polished wooden floors, white-railing staircase, huge open living space with a fireplace just ahead.

"Who could that be?" the quiet female voice spoke from another room.

"Check the door," someone else replied with the air of business.

A woman appeared around the corner, clearly coming from the kitchen. Her hair was pulled back in a low messy bun. She wiped her hands on an apron depicting a bunch of gingerbread men. Breaking into a huge dimpled smile, she cried, "It's Paxton. Pax is home!"

He scooped her up in an enormous hug. "Hi, Mom!"

"What were you doing out there in that storm? We were worried about you!" She looked him over as though making sure he was okay.

"Paxton?" An older man, probably Paxton's dad, came around the corner, the front of his shirt covered in sawdust shavings. "Hey! You made it!"

Paxton hugged his dad too, and Kate fiddled with the handle of her luggage. The awkwardness of the situation seeped into her like the warmth from the house. She didn't belong here. She didn't even want to be here.

"And who's this?" his mom asked, coming over politely.

"Uh." Paxton jumped over to stand by her. "It's just… Kate."

She nodded in what she hoped was a professional way. "Your son was just driving me home for Christmas."

"He didn't say anything to us!" his mom cried.

Kate saw instantly that she had misinterpreted her words. "No, I—"

"It's perfectly fine. I'm glad you came. Come on, would you like a gingerbread cookie? They just came out of the oven."

Part of Kate melted. She would think of a way out of this as soon as she had a cookie. "Sure." She followed the woman into her big kitchen. The cookie sheet sat on a marble island, the little men perfectly cut out.

Paxton's mom untied her apron and drew it over her head before scooping up a cookie with the spatula. "Here you go!"

"Thank you, Mrs. Jones." Despite herself, she smiled.

His mom hung up the apron and looked back toward the front door. "What was that noise?" From in the other room —Kate would have guessed on the stairs—came a new voice, a woman's. Children chattering and running followed right behind it.

"May!" she heard Paxton say. Kate headed back through the kitchen with his mother. Paxton and a tall woman with his dark wavy hair rocked back and forth in a hug.

When he let her go, she said, "I didn't think you'd be back until later!"

"I didn't think so either, but the storm kind of messed with my plans."

"Who's this?" The new, younger woman echoed their mother's question.

"Kate. Kate, this is my sister May."

Kate wiped her hand off on her jeans before shaking May's hand.

A little girl, maybe five years old, ran up to her like a golden retriever and stared at the cookie in her hand. "Are the cookies ready?" she cried.

Kate looked at Paxton's mom, who crouched down to the level of the five-year-old and little three-year-old boy who seemed to materialize out of thin air. "The cookies are ready. Do you want one?"

"Yes!" they yelled, almost in unison, running to the kitchen.

Paxton laughed. "It's weird that they're so big now."

"I know!" said May. "Time goes so fast. And you haven't visited since… when was it?"

Paxton pursed his lips. "It's been a few months."

"How's life in Chicago?"

His mother stepped in with his father. "Let's go into the living room instead of standing in the hallway." She shepherded them toward the fireplace. Garlands with Christmas lights draped across the mantle and a large Christmas tree stood in the corner, covered in ornaments. A banner with a vintage-looking Santa hung on the wall. Coca-Cola certainly did a bang-up job with that ad campaign in the 20's. Even the throw pillows had jingle bells or sleighs or candy canes on them. Little touches of Christmas were everywhere.

"I'm going to finish what I was doing," Paxton's dad said. "It's good to have you back. When you get the chance, you should see my new project. I could use your help."

"Yeah, I'll be there in a sec," Paxton said, sinking into a fluffy cream-colored couch. May sat in the adjacent matching armchair.

Seconds later, the two kids ran through the room. "Can we go and play upstairs?"

"Just be careful," May said, and up the stairs they went with their cookies in hand.

Kate bit off the arm of her cookie, wondering where to sit. She settled on the other end of the couch. Paxton's mother sat in the mirrored armchair next to her.

"Dad is working on another dresser," May explained. "The Gottlieb family asked for it. Jason is going to surprise his wife with it." A shadow passed over her face.

"Oh, that's really nice," Paxton said, taking his sister's hand for a second. "I don't know why he wants my help though."

"You've always been good at that," his mother said. "He needs your eye for detail."

"I'll see it in a little bit."

His mother turned so she could face Kate. "So, how long have you two known each other?"

Kate almost choked on the gingerbread man's head. There was no mistaking what she meant.

Paxton spoke as she coughed. "Not very long," he said.

She glared at him, unable to get the tickle out of her throat. *Aren't you forgetting something? That we aren't together?*

"Will you be here for Christmas, Kate?"

She shook her head helplessly as another fit of coughing shook her.

"No," Paxton said, laying his strong hand on her shoulder. Who did he think he was? Why was he pretending like this? "Her family lives in Moscow, so I need to drop her off there tomorrow."

"Oh," May cooed at Kate. "At least you get to come for a little bit. Christmases here are the best."

"The best," Paxton echoed, smiling.

His mother stood. "Let me get you some milk, honey."

"Thanks," Kate managed through gasping coughs.

A thump sounded from upstairs. "Oh, better check on that." May was up and gone in an instant.

Kate's coughing subsided enough for her to talk. "What was that?" she demanded in a whisper.

"What was what?" he asked innocently.

"Here you go!" His mother glided back into the family room with the milk. "Doing better?" she asked, handing Kate the glass.

"Yes," she said sullenly.

Again, his mother didn't understand the reason for Kate's reaction. She shook her head sympathetically. "That storm really is bad. Well, just snuggle in and make yourself comfortable." She cast a glance at the crackling fireplace.

Kate had to admit that sounded nice after being so tense in the car. But there was no time. She didn't know these people, especially Paxton, who seemed to be warming up to her far too quickly. "Thanks, that sounds good. Pax, why don't you see what your dad is doing and I'll just get some work done here?" She fluttered her eyelashes, hoping to make him uncomfortable. She could play too.

He didn't flinch. "Sounds good," he said in his deep voice, rising and smoothing his jeans. "I'll be back in a little bit." And he sauntered toward the kitchen, which must also lead to the garage, or wherever it was that his dad was building the dresser.

"I'll let you relax," his mother said. "Blanket's on the couch if you want it," she added confidentially.

"Thank you." She whipped out her phone and started tearing through work at a rabid pace.

PLAYING PRETEND

Normally when Kate was working, she could drown out all distractions around her—get in the zone—but after a while, she started noticing a sound like wooden blocks being thrown against the house. She tossed the blanket aside and peered out the glass door beside the fireplace. Through the swirling snow, she saw Paxton chopping firewood.

This was her chance to set the record straight with him. No one in their right mind would go outside in a snowstorm (except him, apparently) so they could talk alone.

She pulled on her jacket and a hat before going outside. Her face stung instantly with cold, but Paxton didn't seem to feel it. In fact, it looked like he'd worked up a bit of a sweat chopping those logs.

"Paxton!" she hissed.

He didn't hear her.

"Paxton!" she said a bit more loudly.

He turned around and smiled before setting another fat log on the block. He swung and it fell perfectly in two. It was kind of impressive.

"What's up?" he asked.

She stood out of ax range. "Well, you're an idiot for standing out in the cold like this," she began.

"Then so are you."

She cleared her throat. "Okay, fine, but I only came out here to talk to you. Why did you let your mom think that we're together?"

"I never lied."

"Neither did I, but she has the wrong idea, don't you think?"

The ax hung blade-down as he straightened up. "I know," he said. "I'm sorry about that. I should have checked to make sure that was okay with you. It's just that my mom has wanted me to find somebody for a long time now and I'm just not the kind of person who dates around, you know?" He set down the ax and gestured with a gloved hand for her to come closer. With tiny steps, she did, and he handed her a piece of firewood. He kept adding to the stack as he talked. "My family's had some huge disappointments the past couple years, and I thought I could at least make Mom's Christmas a little better. I wouldn't take the story too far. Just enough that she'd think I was happy. You'll leave tomorrow and I'd tell her the truth after Christmas." He began carrying an even bigger stack of logs in his own arms. "It's freezing out. Let's go in."

Kate wasn't sure what to say, so she took the armful of wood back through the glass door into the fireplace-warm living room. He showed her where to set the logs clattering and clunking into a nice stack.

"I'm not going to lie to your mom," she whispered.

"I'm not asking you to."

"And don't try anything funny."

"Wouldn't dream of it."

When his mom entered, Kate realized that she and Paxton had been whispering awfully close. She backed away a few inches. "Oh, I didn't mean to interrupt," she said jovially. "Pax, thanks for the firewood. I think we'll be set to weather the storm now!" She looked thoughtfully at Kate. "Have you shown Kate the collection yet?"

"Oh, Mom…"

"You should! Paxton has *enormous* talent." She scrunched her forehead with the word. "Show her! Maybe she can convince you to take yourself seriously."

Despite herself, Kate was intrigued. "What collection?"

"It's…" He looked at the ceiling as though searching for a word. Instead, he settled on brushing the snow and bits of wood from the front of his jacket.

"It's amazing," his mother finished.

"Fine! I'll show her."

His mom clasped her hands together happily. Kate suddenly remembered Paxton's driver mantra: to make each ride special, a personalized experience. He wanted to make Christmas special for his mom.

It was just for one day. Not even one day.

She could pretend to be Paxton's girlfriend.

He headed toward the kitchen where the workroom or garage was, where his dad had gone a couple hours ago. He opened the door for her. She was right—it was a kind of heated garage area, except instead of cars, it looked like a woodshop. The mostly finished dresser stood in a mound of shavings off to the left, but it was the shelves that caught her attention. Tons of intricately carved little figures had been meticulously set in rows. There were chess sets—so many chess sets!—and nativity scenes, as well as figures that didn't seem to belong to a group. She drifted closer. The chess sets were all themed. Light knights fought dark knights, Allied planes fought Axis planes, predators fought prey.

If she hadn't found these sets in a woodshop, she would have thought that they were just a collection. She wouldn't have guessed Paxton made them, but the sheepish look on his face gave him away. "You made all these?" she asked, awestruck as she gestured to all the rows. There must have been five hundred figures.

"Yeah." He rubbed the back of his neck.

"These are incredible!" She picked up a polished horse. Its tail flowed behind it in the wind. Amazing. "Are you selling these?"

"I tried for a while, but there's not much demand around here, and I'm not techie enough to figure out how to send them to bigger cities like St. Louis or Denver."

"Or Chicago? Why didn't you bring them with you?"

"I do bring a few things back every time I visit, but a few sales here and there isn't enough for a living."

"I could help you." The words were out of her mouth before she realized what she was saying. She had enough on her plate already. The account that would earn her the promotion took up all of her time, and she still got nervous that she wouldn't finish everything before the new year. "I mean…"

He waved her offer away. "That's okay. I like doing it anyway, and I've given up on the dream of making this a career a long time ago."

Kate pursed her lips. Paxton could make good money with this. It frustrated her that he couldn't figure out how to find the right clients. Surely these chess sets could go for three hundred a pop to the right people. And the nativity scenes. Many people liked Christmas enough to put those out every year, and were willing to spend a pretty penny for a good set.

"Hey, it's all right." He must have sensed her frustration. Flashing a smile, he opened the door to the house again.

Guilt gnawed behind her belly button as she ascended a couple stairs to the kitchen. She really could help him, and it wouldn't even take much time. She gave a little sigh as she made up her mind. There was no time for this, but his collection couldn't just sit there. Paxton's blue eyes had glowed with pride when he looked at what he'd made. Despite the inconvenience of today and inevitable inconvenience of tomorrow when she pulled together a small marketing platform for him, he had been kind to her. She might as well be kind back.

She turned at the door. Paxton stood at the bottom of the two stairs. They were eye to eye. Close again, as they had been by the fireplace.

"I'd like to help," she said.

"You're busy with other things," he said, dismissing her offer again. He tried to head into the house.

She blocked his way. "Really. I would."

He rocked back and regarded her. A hint of a smile tugged at his mouth. Finally, he raised his eyebrows in pleased resignation. "All right. You're a high-powered marketing exec. If you want to help me, that's great." He nodded. "Thank you."

The warmth in his eyes made her warm too. She cleared her throat and moved so he could get into the kitchen. "If you could just send me high-quality pictures of the best pieces, I could get started."

"Will do," he said cheerfully. He grabbed a gingerbread man on the way to the living room. Before he disappeared through the opening, he cast her a knowing look. "Thank you, Kate, for everything."

*T*he day passed more quickly than Kate would have expected. She didn't play up the fake girlfriend thing, but she didn't deny it now either. She spent most of the afternoon holed away somewhere in the house, trying to answer client questions, set up ads, and fend off Maureen.

May's little girl Rachel rushed into the guest room. "Come on!" she cried. "We're doing Christmas carols!"

"I don't really sing," Kate said nicely, hoping that would make her go away.

"Come on!" Rachel grabbed her hand. "*Everybody* sings carols.

It's Christmastime." Then she gave one of those Puss-in-Boots stares that not even the strongest could resist.

And she had agreed to go along with Paxton's pretend relationship. A real girlfriend would probably swallow the stage fright that hollowed out her stomach even as she walked down the stairs with Rachel. Piano music filtered up.

May, Davy (the little boy), and his parents all stood around a baby grand that stood in the corner of the big living room. Paxton sat at the bench playing incorrect versions of jingle bells. Davy was doubled over laughing. "That's not 'Jingle Bells!'" he screamed.

"Oh, you mean this?" Paxton played a low, somber version with a face to match.

"No!"

"Then how does it go?"

May prompted him. "Jingle bells, jingle bells…"

"Jingle all the way!" Davy finished the line with gusto.

"Oh!" Paxton pretended to remember the song. "Like this?" His fingers danced over the keys as he played a surprisingly nice version of the song Kate had grown up hating.

Rachel ran to give her mother a hug. Mr. Jones, his hand on Mrs. Jones' shoulder, smiled when he saw Kate. "I'm glad you came down," he said. "I know you're busy with whatever it is, but caroling is a tradition in our house."

"We do it every year!" Rachel said, taking her mom's hand.

"Paxton started the tradition," Mrs. Jones said, almost confidentially.

Kate wasn't sure what to say. "Oh, okay."

Paxton cracked his knuckles. He'd rolled his sleeves up to his elbows. She hadn't realized how strong his arms were. "Let's start with something easy," he said, resting his fingers on the keys. "Rachel, do you know 'Silent Night'?"

"She sure does," May answered.

He played a little flourish and began a simple version of the song Kate had heard a million times. The whole family, including Paxton, sang along to the first verse. The whole scenario felt like a Hallmark card. But it was sweet. Paxton's resonating baritone was particularly nice to listen to.

When that song ended, he twisted to look up at her. Something in her gut flipped over. "Kate, you should sing with us."

"I don't have a good voice like you guys."

"It doesn't matter. It's just for the fun of it."

She prayed he wouldn't push her.

"How about this one?" He snatched a pair of Harry Potter prop glasses from the piano shelf—had they been there the whole time?—and popped them on his nose. They were clearly made for a child, and she wondered if they were Davy's. Paxton could barely see out the little circles. The kids giggled. Harry Potter with scruff. She didn't remember that in any of the movies.

He played a chord. "So this is Christmas," he sang. "What have you done? Another year over, a new one just begun…"

The glasses suddenly made sense. John Lennon.

She blushed as she realized he did this all for her. He paused the song to try to teach the kids the part children sing in the original song: "War is over…" It was too complicated for them, but he soldiered on with those ridiculous glasses. When his niece and nephew failed to catch on, she hummed the children's part while he sang the main melody.

When he played the final chord, he looked up at her again. Even through the glasses, there was such warmth in that look that she felt it on her face. The family clapped. He pulled off the prop glasses and set them back on the piano.

"See, you can sing!" his mother said.

"I was humming, not singing," Kate said, but she was pleased anyway.

The afternoon wore away with other Christmas traditions that Kate was duty-bound to participate in. She kept her phone in her back pocket so she could chip away at her tasks, earn her promotion, with any spare minute.

The day had been so dark with the storm that she didn't notice the sun was going down until it was completely black outside. Paxton would check the roads first thing in the morning and they would set off as soon as possible. Moscow was only a little over an hour away, and she had to get back with plenty of time left before Brian's engagement.

The kids went to bed around eight. May, tuckered out, stayed upstairs after that. Shortly thereafter, Mr. and Mrs. Jones turned in to watch CSI in their room before going to sleep.

That left Kate and Paxton, nursing their second hot toddy in front of the fire. They sat closer than they had that morning, in order to fool his mother. He'd even slung one arm around the back of the couch behind her. But when she left, they hadn't moved.

Kate closed both hands around her glass, feeling the warmth seep into her skin. "That John Lennon thing earlier... that was nice. Thank you."

"Yeah, I just borrowed Davy's glasses. Thought you might like that."

"You really seem to like it here. So why did you move? I'm sure you could at least make a living." She hoped it didn't sound rude.

He looked down. "Yeah, I could. I was. It would be nice to stay here, but I was trying to save up."

"For what?" She took an expectant sip.

He ran his free hand through his dark, wavy hair. "I... So, about a year ago, May's husband Ralph walked out on her and the kids." His eyes darkened. "He made all the money, so she was forced to move back in with my parents. My parents don't mind," he added quickly, "but she really needs a place of her own. She's working now, but at this rate, she'll still be stuck here a long time, even though real estate is pretty cheap around here."

Kate looked at the baby grand on the far side of the room. The radiating fire sizzled.

"You can find a small house for a fraction of what it would cost in Chicago," he continued. "So, a couple months after Ralph left, I moved out there to try to save up just a down payment—get her back on the right foot." He waved his hand as though the down payment for a house was no big deal.

She wheeled on him. "You're saving up a *house payment?*"

He retreated to his hot toddy and shrugged. "What about you?" he asked into his glass. His voice echoed strangely.

It was probably the alcohol, but she didn't mind sharing the story. "I didn't really like living in Moscow growing up. My family's okay, but the town is so small." She swallowed. "I met this guy and he lived in Chicago. So when I finished up my degree, I moved out there to be with him. He changed out there, though. He was much more about himself than about me—always at work events and parties and… other girls' houses."

"What was his name?" He moved closer. Their hips touched.

"Jasper."

"Jasper?" A smile tugged at his lips. "He sounds like a movie villain."

"I know, I know." But the memory was still surprisingly painful. She never talked about him.

They let the quiet sit for a moment. Then he prompted, "So you stayed."

"I did," she said, squaring her shoulders. The motion made her back touch his arm, but she didn't mind. He closed his hand around her shoulder. Like two teenagers in a theater. "I got an amazing job. And I'm up for a promotion. Did I tell you that?" She faced him, and his face was very close to hers. Her heart stopped for a second, and she turned back to look at the fire.

"I don't think you did. That explains all the work you've been doing."

"Yes, I have to finish everything by New Year's. It's a lot."

"Do you think you'll be able to get it all done?"

"If I have Dramamine."

He laughed quietly. "And silence, probably."

She nodded, turning back to him. He was close enough to kiss her. Her breathing shallowed as she saw his eyes move from her eyes to her lips and back. One side of his face glowed with firelight. Slowly, his arm tightened around her shoulder, drawing her closer. She didn't need the encouragement. She leaned into him and brought her lips to his.

MOSCOW

Kate wasn't sure what to think the next morning. She knew she liked Paxton. From the late-night kisses, she had a pretty good idea that Paxton liked her. They kept finding each other's gaze, drawn like magnets. Every time she caught him looking at her, her insides flipped over. It was like being back in high school. She hadn't felt this way in so long. Part of her was giddy and the other part confused. Was this too good, too sudden, to be true?

She wouldn't jeopardize her job to be with him, but they could pretend a little longer. She forced the thought of the promotion to the back of her mind. She wouldn't worry about that today. It was Christmas Eve, her brother was getting engaged, and she was falling for a handsome stranger. Just let the day be good.

By nine o' clock the next morning, the snow had melted enough to get back on the roads again. Admittedly, it was slow going. Patches of black ice made everything treacherous, but at least they could leave. The Jones family seemed sad to see Kate go. It was an odd feeling. She knew most of her co-workers, but most of them didn't care when she left (Lucy excepted.)

Mrs. Jones gave her a hug and she gave Rachel and Davy high fives before she zipped her purple coat to leave. "Come back soon!" said Paxton's mom.

Kate gave her a big smile. She couldn't make any promises, but she hoped she could come back soon. She slipped her hand in Paxton's big, strong one and gave it a squeeze.

The dimple appeared on his cheek. "We'd better go," he said. "Mom, May."

They walked to the car. The front door shut behind them, the wreath swinging a little on its hook. Paxton got in first and leaned awkwardly to open the passenger door from the inside. She smiled as she slid into the seat beside him.

He raised his eyebrows at her. "They liked you, you know."

"Oh, well, of course," she teased. "They seem really nice."

"They're great."

They spent next ten minutes laughing and trying to figure out the lyrics to "Across the Universe." Kate even tried singing. He found out just how tone deaf she was, but she didn't care as much about that as she had before.

An hour or so later, they passed the sign for Moscow, Ohio. It lived up to its name just then. Freezing cold and covered in snow, it looked like it could be somewhere in Russia. "Okay, put in your address," Paxton said, handing her his phone.

Phone.

She had fallen behind in her work. She hadn't done any since yesterday afternoon. Her shoulders tightened at the thought. Could she finish in time? It would be a close finish, if she could pull it off at all. She punched in her parents' address.

"Here you go," she said, distracted again.

"What's the matter?"

"Nothing."

"I think it's something."

"I've never met Brian's girlfriend."

He patted her hand. "I'm sure she's great. You trust your brother, right?"

"Most of the time."

He side-eyed her as though he could tell that something else was bothering her, but he didn't keep prying. They eased off the freeway onto her exit. A thought struck her. "Are you staying to meet everybody?"

"Do you want me to?"

She was quiet.

He bit his lip, sensing her indecision. His blue sweater brought out his eyes. "We're not… really—"

"Right, not really," she said quickly.

"Do you want me to take you back in a few days?"

It was odd. They had never talked about it. "Yes, please."

"When?" His tone had shifted. Still polite, but something upset him.

"I know you want to spend the holidays with your family. When are you going back?"

"I wasn't planning to go back until January second."

Her blood froze. "I can't do that. I have to get back sooner. The twenty-sixth if possible."

"You'll only be there for Christmas Day?"

"And tonight. That's plenty of time. Can you go the day after Christmas?"

He flexed his strong jaw. "I wish I had known when you were coming back. Maybe you can find someone else."

She hated the idea of riding with some stranger. Paxton wasn't a stranger anymore. Why didn't he want to take her? "Pax," she said, sensing him slip away. She hadn't been this drawn to anyone since Jasper.

"My family needs me this time of year," he said, braking at a stoplight. "It's the first time off I've taken in months." He looked at her. "But I want to drive you in January."

"If I waited that long, I wouldn't get the promotion."

"You could get it later."

"You don't understand."

"I like you, Kate."

Her stomach dropped. She liked him too, but she wasn't about to blow a huge opportunity for a man she just met, even if he did have broad shoulders and a snow-melting gaze. Couldn't she have both?

A car honked behind them. The light had turned green.

They were silent for the next few minutes until he pulled up in her parents' driveway.

"I'll see you back in Chicago," she said.

"I'm not sure that's the best idea."

"What?" Was he the kind of guy who couldn't handle a high-powered woman who wanted a career as well as a family? "Paxton, what are you talking about?" It was as if their intimate moment the night before meant nothing. But it hadn't meant nothing to her.

"Have a safe trip back," he said, yanking her suitcase out of the back of the Forester.

If he wanted to cut off the possibility of a relationship, she wasn't going to beg. She stood up straighter and took the handle of her luggage from him. "I will. How much do I owe you?"

"It's on me," he said, getting back in the driver's seat.

"But I want to pay you."

"Not for this." He gave her a searing look that made her want to kiss him again. But that ship was long gone. "Okay, take care," he said. With a wave, he backed out and was gone.

She hated herself for watching him go, but she didn't turn to go inside until she couldn't hear his car engine anymore.

The rolling suitcase bumped over the icy driveway and up the stairs to the front door. She knocked and waited.

Mom opened the door. "Oh, sweetie!" she cried. "I texted you an hour ago and you never replied. I got so worried!"

She pulled out her phone to check. She had two unread messages from her mom. "Sorry about that," she muttered.

"Well, come on in and say hi to your brother."

She obeyed. Her brother Brian sat on the oversized tan couch in their little living room. His girlfriend Jessica sat above him on the arm, looking like a Christmas card model in her sparkly red sweater dress. She was far more dressed up than he was. Kate recognized Brian's salmon polo shirt from his senior year at Moscow High.

"Hey!" Brian greeted. A heavy dose of nervousness tinged his grin. Could Jessica see it? Did she know about the coming engagement? Is that why she wore that dress?

Kate let go of the suitcase to shake Jessica's hand, feeling strangely empty. After a few minutes, the family was talking merrily together. Despite being so done up, Jessica seemed nice enough.

The rest of the day passed quickly in a flurry of shopping and snacks and "Feliz Navidad." Brian got more and more antsy until Kate was sure Jessica had to suspect something.

He proposed at the gazebo. It was situated in the middle of downtown, by all the shops with trinkets and consignment clothes. The family gathered around the bottom, as Brian invited Jessica to step inside it with him. The string lights covering the structure bathed them in a warm yellow glow. When he got down on one knee, she certainly acted surprised. She covered her mouth and cried, pretty tears leaking out the side of her eyes. Even Kate's eyes bugged out at the sight of the ring—a huge solitaire.

They all hugged and squealed and welcomed Jessica into the family. Kate felt complicated. Glad for her brother, happy for Jessica, moved by the display of love, regretful about Paxton...

As soon as she was alone in the guest room, she got more work done. The fury of productivity took her mind off Paxton and the non-relationship they'd had—just enough of a taste to bring her loneliness rushing back. With the promotion held out like a carrot, she didn't have time to worry about men right now.

She got so caught up in creating campaigns and replying to the emails that had built up over the past twenty-four hours that she didn't go to bed until 2:00 in the morning.

Eyes as bleary as they had been when Pax had first picked her up at the apartment, she shuffled out of her room on Christmas morning. Brian and his fiancée lived in an affectionate world of their own, always touching noses and gazing longingly.

She felt no compunction about calling a new driver to take her back home to Chicago on the twenty-sixth. It was definitely time to go home.

She had to go back to what she was good at. She had to get that promotion.

"So, I was thinking that we could present this as the new campaign." Kate handed her a laminated document of her work. "Everyone wants individualized service. If the customers can feel that they're getting special treatment, then they'll come back. They'll feel that the company is on their side. So that's what their social media should focus on—interacting with customers as much as providing their own curated feed."

Maureen leafed through the packet impassively, picking up one page at a time with her nail. "This is interesting," she finally said.

Interesting? Was that a good thing? Kate fidgeted under the table.

"This will take a lot of manpower."

"I know," Kate said quickly. "But I think the payoff will warrant the extra work."

"Are you willing to stake your career on that?"

Kate froze. "I think so."

Maureen's face thawed. "Then you've got the promotion." She reached across the table to shake Kate's hand.

The confirmation sent shock waves through her body. The

promotion! The raise and prestige that went with it! She could finally afford her nice place. She'd worked hard and now she was one of the youngest managers in the firm. "I—I do? Thank you! Thank you!" She realized she was on her feet.

Maureen looked at her, amused. "Good work. Now take the night off."

It was New Year's Eve. Kate didn't have any plans, but Lucy had said something about going back to Joey's. She shook Maureen's manicured hand one more time for good measure and practically danced out of the office.

Huge pieces of confetti already littered the floor of the bar when she got there at 11:30. Lucy ran up to her immediately, curled blonde hair bobbing. "I'm so glad you could make it, girl!"

"I got it! I got it, Lucy!"

"What? The promotion?"

She squeaked and nodded her head furiously.

"Oh, Kate, that's great! So proud of you. Let's get you something to celebrate! Bartender!" she shouted. "A round of champagne!"

The bottle came and they clinked their tall glasses together.

Lucy almost choked on her first sip. She held a dainty hand to her mouth and rushed past Kate to the door. "Mark!" she heard her say.

Kate turned to see them locking lips by the door. So that was still going well. She waited a minute to see if Lucy would come back. For a while, she didn't. Kate gazed around the bar and realized that everyone had come with someone else—mostly significant others, but some had groups of friends.

She peeked at her phone. Paxton never sent the photos of his woodshop collection.

The TVs in the corners showed the ball in Times Square. A hitch in the party atmosphere meant that midnight was almost here. Everyone fluffed up like birds in a bath. The group of girls at the end of the bar straightened their silvery hats and sleek dresses. Mark and Lucy, their arms around each other, turned to the screens.

One of the bartenders announced that they were only a minute away from the new year. There was some drunken cheering. Servers rushed around to refill the champagne toasts.

"Ten, nine, eight...!" Everyone shouted the numbers as the ball dropped. "Three, two, one!" Noise blowers honked, people screamed and cheered, confetti dropped from somewhere, and couples kissed each other. "Happy New Year!"

Kate held up her glass and downed the champagne.

Lucy and Blond Beard Mark stood nose to nose, too much like Brian and Jessica had on Christmas. A wave of disappointment swept over her, unconnected to work. That part of her life fulfilled her. Almost every part of her, but she wanted someone else to tell about her personal victory, and there was no one. She sat on the barstool she had used the other night when she had needed a ride home...

The person next to her stood up and she heard someone say, "Is this seat taken?"

She knew that voice. Paxton. He showed up behind her dressed in a blue button-up, silver tie, and black slacks. He looked really good. Like, really good.

"Someone was sitting there a second ago," she said, unsure what else to say or assume.

"I made him move," he replied, sitting down next to her. A whiff of cologne hovered around him.

"I thought you weren't supposed to be back for another few days."

"I wasn't. But then I thought, I really like this girl. I shouldn't be so stubborn. I can be really stubborn."

"Yes, you can."

"And so can you."

"Well—" He fixed her with a look. "Okay, fine. I can be stubborn too." Looking into his handsome face, with its five o' clock shadow and strong jaw and deep eyes and wavy hair, she almost lost herself. But she still wasn't sure why he was here. She couldn't lose her head. "I thought you wanted to be with your family."

"I do. I'm going back to visit in a couple weeks. I'm going to try to visit once a month now instead of waiting so long."

With their barstools twisted toward each other, their knees touched. "That's great. I'm sure May will appreciate that."

"I think so."

"Did you give her… you know? The house?"

He ran a hand through his hair. "Not yet, but it should only take about four more months." He held up crossed fingers.

"Oh, she'll be so happy." She reached for her purse. "I really should pay you for part of the ride at least. For May."

He started to protest until she said his sister's name. She handed him five twenties and he handed back four. "For May," he said. "Really, though, I didn't mind it. Not at all by the end. You were good company."

She felt they were on dangerous ground, so she didn't respond.

He changed the topic. He always was good at personalizing the situation. "So, did you get it? The promotion?"

Her face split into a smile. "Yes! My boss just told me before I came here."

"Congratulations!" He went to hug her and thought twice. "I'm glad. You worked really hard on that."

"Yeah." Inside, she stilled. "You helped with that, actually."

"Me? How?"

She swallowed, feeling vulnerable. "I saw the way you make each ride special and you treat each member of your family so specifically and thoughtfully, and I thought, that should be the direction of the campaign. You know, personalizing each experience. Everyone wants to feel special, like they're wanted."

He lowered his head a little. "Even you?"

There was that blush again. Just when she thought she was free of this. She cleared her throat. "Of course."

His gambit didn't work, so he changed the subject again. "I've decided to sell those carvings after all."

A well of happiness bubbled up at the thought. He needed to show the world his handiwork. "Oh, that's great!"

"I thought you'd be glad. Just have to get a website up and going. Then I can split my time between Chicago and home."

Home. He said the word so easily. She didn't have memories of her home that were quite as fond. But in a strange way, she did miss his family's house. "Good."

"Okay, in case you haven't gotten it yet, I came back here for you. You've reminded me how good home is, but how it can be even better. I've been looking after people my whole life and forgot to look after myself. So I asked myself, what do I want this year? And the only answer was… you."

"That's silly," she said automatically. "We just—"

"What do you want?"

She was looking at it. But wasn't this too rash?

His dimple appeared again. It must have been the look in her eyes. He stood and gave her his rough hand to help her to her feet. "I know I'm a little late, but this is New Year's Eve, isn't it?"

"New Year's Day."

"Close enough." He took her face in his hands and kissed her. The bar disappeared. The sounds went silent. There was only Paxton holding her close.

When she emerged back into the world, she saw him smiling above her, and, just past him, Lucy giving her a thumbs up. Lucy wouldn't have to call her a ride tonight. With a full heart, she wrapped her arms around Paxton and laid her head on his chest. No, she was already home.

LEXI AND THE CHRISTMAS BREAKUP

TANNER

This was going to be just like the end of a Hallmark movie.

Lexi sighed as she gripped the steering wheel, watching rows of dark pine trees rush by on either side of her Toyota Camry. As soon as she met Tanner in college, she knew he was the one. A carpenter, rough without being rude, masculine without showing off. He was just getting over a breakup and needed a friend, he said. She was more than happy to become that friend. Several group dates later, they were official, and he said he'd never want to move back to Colorado but would rather spend all his time with her at OSU.

Of course Lexi didn't want to stay in Columbus forever. It was a quaint town with wild football to soothe even the most rabid fan, but she wanted a different life. Maybe something with more air. More mountain air.

Feeling indulgent, she rolled the window down and icy wind went ripping through the car. She shivered, smiled, and pushed the button again.

He would be so surprised.

He *had* invited her, of course. They'd been dating for nine months so it was about time she met his family. The glimpse of them she'd gotten at graduation a few months ago wasn't enough, but it was promising.

His father wore jeans and a blazer and had an easy smile on his face when his son's name was called with the rest of the biology majors. Beside him, his mother cheered, looking ten years younger than she really was, but she didn't look like she'd had work done. It must be something about living in the outdoors that made a person seem fresher. Tanner had a younger brother too, still in high school, a senior now, who was surprisingly fun to talk to.

With Christmas around the corner, she would get to spend quality time with the people who would soon be her in-laws. She hoped. She assumed.

She cast her mind back to all the rom-coms she had binged with her best friend as she prepared for this trip. Every one of those heroines felt nervous just before the end. But then the kiss came, the confetti rained down, dancing broke out, and everyone left feeling celebratory and loved.

Life wasn't like a rom-com, she rationalized… but what if it could be? She still lay awake some nights thinking how lucky she was to have found Tanner Bingham. They were each other's confidants, and his dreamy looks didn't hurt either.

After a string of men who treated her casually—not badly, per se, but casually—she had started to retreat from the notion that she could ever find that love that twists your stomach and makes you jump into the unknown. Good enough was good enough. Until Tanner.

She blew out a breath. The ghost of a cloud formed, but the air blasting from the heater dispersed it.

Today was the day she would tell him she loved him.

She hadn't used those words since high school, and that, she told herself, was only practice. She hadn't really loved those boys. Those were infatuations, little crushes. Tanner was a man she could marry, and he deserved to know how happy he'd made her.

The mountain road was so picturesque. It was a pity it wasn't snowing. *How romantic would that be?* She pictured little ice crystals clinging to her hair as she found him in his hometown just before Christmas. The image was as sweet and warm as a cup of hot chocolate.

Smiles chased over her lips as her thoughts ran faster. She could use a distraction, or a funnel to catch all these thoughts. She flicked on the radio. Breakup song. New channel. Breakup song. *Why are there so many breakup songs?*

If the road weren't so twisty, with puddles of black ice, she could dig around in her purse for her phone and its collection of better love songs. As it was, she had to sit back and let Taylor Swift talk about last Christmas and how the day after didn't go so well.

Soon enough, she started singing along. Good thing no one else was in the car. She had her skill set. Anthropology or being an office secretary, depending on who you asked. Singing wasn't in it.

Maybe it would snow after all. The sky was a low white over the black trees, as perfect as a Bob Ross painting. Little mountain towns snuck up on her. Any moment now, one of these bends would reveal Tall Pine, CO.

She pulled her red scarf away from her throat distractedly. This was really happening. She was really going to say it.

As the clouds darkened, glittering snowflakes began to fall. Tiny ones, a testament to how cold it was outside.

Lexi bit her lip. This was too perfect! Like the ending of *White Christmas* when the general opened the barn door. The warmth that settled in her belly felt like all the Christmas picture books she had grown up with, and the lights they put on the tree. It was magic.

He was magic.

The road curved around another rocky corner. There it was! Tall Pine looked just as charming as she had pictured. The lights she felt within graced all the trees along the main street. She half expected a horse and carriage to go trotting by. Shops with clothes and gifts and handmade foods slid past in squares of orange light.

She slowed the car to a stop along the curb. Pulling a glove off one hand, she fished in her purse for her phone. At first she'd considered making Tanner's brother Jesse a co-conspirator, but thought better of it. What if he couldn't keep a secret? So she'd set it up so that she could track his location on her phone.

His little blue dot wasn't far away. Her ribcage felt tight. She pulled down the sunshade and checked her face in the little mirror. Her light skin looked a little flushed. She fluffed her short hair out of the scarf and fixed her dangling earrings so they faced forward. That was fine. She looked fine.

Now that the moment had come, her legs felt a little wobbly. She could just hear the words coming out of her mouth. "Your face is good. I've come early. So, I love you. Do you love me?" Inane.

She flexed her fingers in a self-soothing gesture and then got out of the car. The slamming door sounded louder than she expected. The noise almost made her jump. Striding down the street in her calf-high boots, she followed the blinking dot to a restaurant. Or a bar. It looked like a bar. A wave of relief flowed over her. What if he had been at a family dinner at home? Or on a construction site? It wouldn't have been so bad, but a public place like this felt right.

The wind blew her snowflake-dusted hair across her cheeks.

It was time.

A long, brown counter covered the back wall of the bar. Behind it sat rows of booze bottles, some of them decorated with garlands or Santa koozies for Christmas. Round tables were scattered across the rest of the floor. It smelled like beer and peanuts but didn't look too much like a dive. It was a Wednesday night, so the place wasn't very busy. Even if it had been, she would have noticed Tanner's oversized blue jacket right away. She'd held it, her hands tucked in the crook of his arm. His brown hair was dry, so he'd been here for a while.

He sat at the bar facing a woman. His shoulders hunched a little in her direction as they talked. She was young and wore a long-sleeve T-shirt with AC/DC on it. Her hair twisted away from her temples, the two strands bound at the back of her head with what looked like a neon rubber band. She looked familiar.

And her hands. Her hands lay on the countertop, occasionally gesturing, but always facing Tanner, like a high schooler on a date at the movies. Available.

Well, this man was not available.

Then one of his hands moved. Lexi stopped.

Something quiet in her said to wait another second.

He swiveled his barstool to face the young woman head on. The angle gave Lexi the full advantage of his profile: that strong jaw and cheek so lean it looked almost sunken in certain lights. The strange woman leaned forward, offering her face for a kiss. He gave her a toothy smile as his hand moved from the countertop to caress her thigh.

Lexi's face went cold, but not from the weather. The humid air inside the bar, the bloodless realization of what was happening, and her strangling sweater all combined until she practically had a fever. At first her feet wouldn't move.

But when they did, oh boy.

She stomped over to the counter. The noise alerted the two of them before she reached the bar. Tanner's hand snapped back as though it had reached into a viper's nest. He stood up to greet her, but the other woman slumped almost imperceptibly against the bar, disappointed.

Now that Lexi saw her close up, she recognized her. They'd

never met in person, but she had seen the girl's picture, handed to her by an emotional Tanner. His ex.

How *could* he?

"Lex!" he said, a little too loudly, scooping her up in a hug before she could move away. Holding her at arm's length, he looked into her face with that dark gaze that made it seem like no one else was in the room. But someone else *was* in the room. "I thought you were coming tomorrow. What are you doing here?"

Tears started in her eyes. She sniffed, playing off the inevitable redness of her face as the effect of cold. "I…"

I'm here to tell you I love you.

SANTA

*N*ow she had no purpose here, she realized, flicking a glance at the other woman. Weakness settled in her limbs as the ramifications of his wandering hand started to topple over like dominoes, one by one by one.

Tanner had said no, he didn't love her, before saying anything at all.

He thought their relationship was just casual too. She was a rebound.

She had driven far, far across the country and now had no business to be in Colorado at all.

Oh God, where will I stay tonight?

None of this came out in words as she looked at him. The girl, who still hadn't stood, turned more conspicuously toward the counter, almost as though she were going to order something. She didn't. It was her attempt at looking nonchalant. Or smug. At that moment, with red rage replacing Lexi's clammy fever, the girl definitely looked smug.

Her throat seized up as she tipped her head back to look at him. She stepped back, putting herself on a more equal footing. Words tumbled through her head, but not out her mouth.

His look shifted from cautiously joyful to nervous around the edges. The worry showed in the way he searched her face in a furtive way and the edges of his eyes crinkled.

"Can I get you anything?" It was the bartender. She wore a tank top and had Miyazaki movie scenes tattooed all up her right arm. Her close-cropped platinum hair, shorter than Lexi's long bob, framed her white face. So much white made her look like an elf or a ghost.

"No," Lexi managed. The bartender strode past to wash glasses in the sink below the counter.

When she looked back at Tanner, his realization had finally written itself all over his face. "It's good to see you," he said, but now his voice was strained beneath the jollity. He half-turned to AC/DC girl. "This is my friend Angie."

Lexi merely hummed, tight-lipped, as she regarded Angie. She knew her name. She'd remembered it as soon as she approached the bar top. It was a name Tanner had talked about in her dorm room, had nearly cried about. This girl had broken his heart. Lexi had pieced it together again, trying to find the man he was before the heartache. And now he was back with her.

Maybe he held on to a sliver of hope that she hadn't seen his hand move.

"We were just catching up," he said. "We used to be close in high school and it's been a while since we've seen each other, so..." His explanations sounded like excuses and they soon petered out. One of the most painful things was that he *was* explaining, as though Lexi were not his closest friend.

She took a deep, barely shuddering breath through her nose to steady herself. The sickly sweet smell of hops and wheat and sugar made her slightly nauseated. She shook her head.

Tanner reached for her hand, but she slipped out of his grip. "No, that's it," she said. "This is over."

For a moment, the sadness in his beautiful eyes matched her own.

Everyone made mistakes. Maybe he didn't mean it…

All the voices of those who told her she was worth more crashed in, a cacophonous choir in her ears.

She could never go back to him after this.

"What?" he asked, the sadness giving way to denial or fake confusion or something.

Lexi looked pointedly at Angie, then back at him. At those eyes that used to look at her and make her feel special, as though she weren't a pit stop on the way to true love, but the thing itself.

She couldn't stay here anymore.

Without answering, she turned around and headed back toward the door. Would he chase her? *Could* he, with his ex, now not ex, watching?

Yanking the door open, she stepped onto the icy street. Cold air blasted across her face, colder after the inside warmth. The Christmas lights grew blurry around the edges, becoming huge globes of haze. A sob ripped from her chest. Against her better judgment, she glanced back. Just an empty street.

She slowed as she tromped back toward her car. *Where am I going?* It was too late to drive back down the mountain. She would have to find a place to stay here in Tall Pine. She grimaced, baring her teeth at the thought. The front of her teeth dried out cold from the winter air.

Looking around, exhausted with grief and driving, she spotted a wooden bench sitting against the wall of shops. Dollar store wreaths hung from the armrests on either side. She slumped onto it, burying her face in her gloved hands. More tears came, but at least there was almost no one walking along the street to notice.

To go from excitement about the future to devastation, from love to heartbreak, from trust to betrayal in one day was almost too much.

Her mind buzzed, trying to rationalize, to see a way out. But what did that even mean? Did she want to get back together with

Tanner? Not after he dated Angie behind her back. So what did she want? To be loved, just to be loved. And now that wouldn't happen—if it did at all—for a long, long time.

She set her mouth in a grim line and sat up. A streak of red unrelated to her pain smudged the edge of her vision. Looking over, she saw a man dressed as Santa trundling over to her. He was the stereotypical large white man with a large white beard and a velvet red coat tied with a large black-buckled belt. The man fit the part with almost startling accuracy. His eyes even seemed to twinkle a little as the black boots got closer.

"Well, are you all right?" he asked. His voice was deep and fruity, exactly as Santa's should be. But it didn't sound like a gimmick or a commercial, but almost as though she were his daughter or a child sitting on the real Santa's lap. It was the kind of voice that seemed to speak solely in advice, but that nobody minded because it was good advice. He bent down over her, not condescending or creepy, but just enough to make it seem like she was the only person in the world.

That focus and attention made her want to trust him. Trust was a strong word, too easily broken. She wanted to listen to him. That was it.

"No," she answered miserably, feeling the lump in her throat rise up again. A tear leaked out of one eye.

"Oh," he said, a noise more than a word. It was an oddly comforting sound.

"Do you want to sit down?" She gestured to the seat next to her.

"All right then—"

"—Unless you have somewhere to be." How presumptuous of her to think that this man wanted to sit and talk to her! He was dressed as Santa, for crying out loud. Obviously he had places to be.

He settled onto the bench in a kind, expansive way. "No, no," he lied reassuringly. She almost believed him. "So what's wrong?"

Did she really want to talk about it… *all* of it? "I'm from out of town and my accommodations just fell through," she said, feeling the formality of her words. "Do you know of a hotel or something around here?"

Her thoughts wandered to her purse and the money in it. *Thanks a lot, student loans,* she thought bitterly, considering how much she could actually afford. Not much.

Santa hummed and looked out into the night sky over the buildings across the street. After plucking a few strands of hair in his beard, he turned back to her. "We don't have many places like that here in Tall Pine. There's a resort down the mountain a bit, or a bed and breakfast you can try. But this is the busy season."

The falling snow seemed to mock her. Snow and Christmas lights and perfect trees made this the busy season. The perfect place to spend time with loved ones for the holidays. She glared at the cheap wreath hanging from her armrest.

"Thank you very much," she said, gathering herself and rising from the bench to walk back to her car.

"Let me know if you find a place," said Santa, de-aging a little in the tone of his voice. It was like a concerned father.

"I'll be fine," she said.

"Well, you know where to find me." Slapping his knees with black-gloved hands, he stood beside her. "What's your name, young lady?"

She hesitated for a second. "Lexi Schmitt," she said. "Have a nice night."

After half an hour of calling the resort, the bed and breakfast, two motels in neighboring towns, and an Air BnB in the area, Lexi came up empty. The resort was too expensive (*who could afford to stay in a place like that?*) and everywhere else was booked for the night. They had no last-minute cancelations.

She sat in the driver's seat with her fist to her lips, thinking. The night was too cold for her to sleep in her car. Red boxy numbers on the dash told her it was 8:56. She could feel her heart beat in her chest. It wasn't going faster than usual, but she could feel it. Maybe the emptiness of this place and the emptiness inside her made the sound echo. Most of the stores had already flipped the sign around that read Closed.

Tanner had tried to call her a few minutes before. Her stomach flipped at the sight of his name, almost as though nothing had changed. But it had. And he had only called once.

She wouldn't panic. There had to be a solution, and that solution was not staying with Tanner's family.

Fueled more by the desire to be proactive than because she thought anything would come of it, she got out of the parked car again. A few stores away, Santa looked like he might be getting ready to leave. His waves to children seemed less jolly. It was possible she was projecting her own emotions. He still beamed just as broadly, deep laugh lines visible above his beard.

He saw her before she thought of something to say. "No luck then?" he asked.

She shook her head.

He looked back up at the sky as though he could tell time there as others could from the sun. He lowered his voice, probably so she wouldn't be embarrassed. "It's getting late. If you just need a place to sleep tonight, I have a spare bedroom."

Normally this offer from a stranger would have disturbed her, but the day had worn her down. Still, she didn't answer right away.

Santa held up his hands. The thick fur edging of his coat floated up with them. Then it was as though he changed his mind about what he was going to say. An impish look crept into his face, and he smiled. "Well, you can bring a taser if it will make you feel more comfortable."

"It would." His disarming attitude made her smile too. She couldn't manage more than a sickly smile, but that was something.

Santa laughed a big belly laugh.

Relief began to creep over her. The idea of staying at Santa's house was odd, and under any other circumstances she wouldn't have considered it, but now it was her only option. At best, she'd get a good story out of it to tell her sister Jessica. At worst, she'd have to beat up an old man. Not a great option. But he seemed all right.

A huge yawn split her face wide open. Her rear was sore from driving all day. She needed some sleep, stat.

"Looks like you're already a little…" His words were cut off by a yawn of his own. "Now look what you're doing to me. All right," he said with a bustling tone of a man planning Christmas secrets, "my house is right over there." He pointed down the street, past the bar. "120 Pinewood Way."

A moment of apprehension gripped her. *What choice do I have?* "Okay," she said, feeling brave.

"Let's go together."

TALL PINE

The next morning, Lexi shot up in bed. Pans clanged and a dog made a half-barking, half-whining noise just outside the door.

Where am I? She looked around the little white room with colored pencil drawings of cabins on the wall, a vase of fake flowers, a window with frilly curtains…

Something tugged at her arm. She jerked away, but the sensation followed her. The strap of her purse. She'd wound it around her arm before going to sleep. Slowly, the horrible events of the night before seeped back into her memory. She sat staring dumbly down at her purse as the pain returned. The bag lay on the blue comforter covered with Thomas the Tank Engine designs, faded and frayed as though it had been washed every week for the past twenty years. Maybe it had been.

"Stacey, no!" she heard Santa say firmly on the other side of the door. Dog nails clicked on hard floors in reply.

Judging from the creaking footsteps, half a dozen people walked through the hallway outside. The guestroom smelled musty with long-faded odors: pine, soap, dirt, and, faintly, cigarettes.

Well, she hadn't been murdered in the night. She ought to thank Santa—*Santa? I should have asked his real name*—before she left town.

After putting on leggings and a sweater dress, and running her fingers through her short hair so it didn't look crazy, she stepped outside. She almost hated the outfit because it was for *him*. Everything she packed had been carefully chosen for a winter wonderland trip of magic and romance. Without Tanner, wearing a good outfit was a waste. At least she wasn't wearing makeup. Puffy eyes fit her mood.

The dark, narrow hallway outside the door had creaky wood floors that announced her arrival long before she could see anyone. Another pan clashed in the kitchen beyond.

A head came into view just for a second. The sandy-haired man peeked comically around the corner with the attitude of someone rushing to prepare baked goods for company. He didn't look angry, or happy, but serious and bustling. She hadn't seen him the night before. For some reason, his presence irritated her. There was another person in the house that she didn't know about? The revelation made her desperate decision last night more embarrassing. But she had no choice now. She had to meet him, or at least come out into the kitchen area.

Emerging from the hallway, she saw Santa (now suit-less), a large gray dog, and the younger man. Maybe it was the mountains, but they all had the air of living by themselves, just like this, men and dog, for a very long time.

"Well, good morning!" said Santa, in the same voice he had used last night. It could be his real voice. The beard was real too. He stood against the sink in a whitish, waffle-knit shirt with the sleeves rolled up.

Sizzling caught her attention. Pancakes?

"Good morning," she replied, although it wasn't.

The sandy-haired man shoved a cupful of syrup into the

microwave and slammed the door shut. The beeping of the buttons stopped the possibility of talking for a moment.

Santa slapped his hands together over the sink as though he were dusting them off and getting ready to go. The dog seemed to think the same thing. It practically danced on its toes, whining faintly as it stared up. Santa ignored it and instead turned to her. "You want coffee before you go?" he asked.

"Okay." His kindness left her feeling oddly resigned, as though fate had landed her there. Fate hadn't done anything. Tanner had put his hand on that girl's leg. She thought of her phone in the other room. Had he called again? He had to have left a text message or two. Even cheaters wouldn't leave her completely in the cold, right?

A hot mug slid across the counter toward her. The steam above the cup looked friendly. She had taken the same kind of tin mug camping when she went on an adventure backpacking trip in middle school. Marshmallows and pony tails and nighttime bonfires came to mind.

She took the mug and sipped gratefully, losing herself in the memory that grew stronger as she smelled the coffee. It tasted good, but it smelled black, bitter, and old, like all self-respecting camp coffee should. Again, the feeling that Santa and his dog lived out here away from civilization in a kind of trapper's paradise flooded over her.

As she scanned the kitchen area, which opened into a small living space by the front door, she noticed that there were very few Christmas decorations. Odd for a man who literally dressed up as Santa. There were three stockings hung on a windowsill and two or three little toy Santas stuffed in corners as though they appeared there by themselves. One belonged between the microwave and the oak cabinets.

A loud alarm announced that the syrup was sufficiently heated. The younger man grabbed the cup out and clanged it on the counter. He still hadn't said hello. Judging from his movements, every task was urgent. Maybe he was late for work. Or maybe he was angry to find a strange woman in his house in the morning.

Lexi retreated to her coffee, which never demanded conversation.

"Pancakes are ready!" Santa announced.

I really need to ask his name. She pointed toward the door. "I should probably be…"

"Well, you should just stay for breakfast, and then you can go wherever you need to be." Something in the twinkle of his eye suggested that he had a good idea why she wanted to get out of town. She was grateful he didn't mention it, if he did know.

"Dad," said the young man quietly, slowing down for the first time, a plate in hand. "If she needs to go…"

So he didn't want her here. The knowledge made her even more uncomfortable. "I can go," she said.

"Sit," said Santa, gently but firmly, setting a plate in front of her on a small round table the same color as the cabinets. "It's the time of good cheer and *hospitality.*"

The younger man pursed his thin lips, but didn't contradict his father. His eyes darted in the swift, active way of someone figuring out a situation. He was tall and lithe, his movements quick and self-assured. As he sat down at the crowded little table, he looked a bit too old to still live in his father's house. He had to be at least twenty-four. Of course, that wasn't quite fair. People lived different lives. It might be almost impossible to find a home in Tall Pine.

Her chest constricted a little at the thought. Briefly, in college, she had looked up Tall Pine on Google Earth, idly searching for a place where she and Tanner could stay when they visited his parents. Really, she had no idea which houses were occupied. Probably all of them.

She crossed her ankles under her seat to avoid bumping knees with either of the two men. A steaming stack of pancakes and the cup of syrup graced the middle of the table already so crammed that she held her coffee cup in one hand just to keep it from taking up space. The dog—*Stacey?*—rushed to the side of the low table as well. It was almost tall enough to put its head on the table as it begged for scraps. No one told it to go away. Personally, she felt crowded.

She waited until the men got their pancakes before she took one for herself. Apart from the coffee, she didn't really want breakfast. She had no appetite. Even a pancake, which under ordinary circumstances she loved, felt gummy and tasteless in her mouth. The syrup helped a little.

"So where are you from?" asked Santa jovially over his pancakes.

"Ohio," she said. "Columbus."

"Ah, very good."

The next logical question would be why she was here, so she turned to the younger man. "I'm Lexi," she said. "I don't think I caught your name."

He gave her a look that said he didn't throw it. The look wasn't hostile, exactly, but wary. As though she wasn't the problem but she *represented* the problem. His features thawed. "Seth," he answered, extending a hand over the table. "Pleased to meet you."

"And I'm Neal," said Santa, laughing in a jolly way as he realized he hadn't introduced himself until now.

She shook their hands and kept trying to eat. Stuffing the last of the breakfast into her mouth, she announced, "I'm leaving, so thanks for giving me a place to stay." She smiled at Neal. "And for the breakfast. I'm just… gonna go home." Heaviness settled in her body as the reality of that sentence hit her. Another long, long drive with enough time for thoughts of the betrayal and the breakup to drive her crazy. It might already be Christmas by the time she got home, unless she hurried.

With renewed urgency, she scraped her chair back from the

table, almost hitting the dog, who had been lying on the floor just behind her seat. She muttered an apology and headed back through the narrow hallway.

❄

She couldn't believe it. Not now. Not today.

The car wouldn't start.

Maybe she had left the interior lights on too long when she had looked up those hotels the night before. In any case, the battery was dead. When she revved the engine, it sounded like an angry cat stuck on a ceiling fan.

Why did she ever think this trip was a good idea?

She laid her forehead on the cold pleather steering wheel, half from misery and half in hiding. This was a tiny town. Tanner could be anywhere, and he would definitely notice her car if he saw it. Parallel parked in plain view. Along the main street.

She groaned loudly, plucking out her phone to check for car repair shops this time, or at least a service that could give her a jump. Randall's Car Shop, Tire World, Brakes by Maude… They each offered the wrong kind of service or were too far away to be effective.

How could people live in this town? How did Tanner grow up here, away from everything?

Santa, in full regalia again, appeared through the passenger window, gesturing for her to roll it down so he could say something. Without power, the button was useless, so she got out of the car and looked at him. "Yes?"

"I thought you'd be long gone by now," he said kindly. "Is there any trouble?"

She swallowed a couple times. "My car won't start. I just need a jump."

He held up one gloved finger and put it to the side of his nose, like it describes in that poem. "Ah, it's like someone doesn't want you to leave."

"I need to get home as soon as possible," she said, as business-like as she could muster. "Do you know someone who can jump the engine?"

"Oh, I'll call Seth. He can do it."

He wouldn't be happy about that, she knew. But beggars couldn't be choosers. She all but rolled her eyes. "All right." The Santa family had been so generous already that her cheeks burned red at having to ask for another favor. She must seem so helpless. A little girl lost in the woods. Not a twenty-two-year-old with an anthropology degree.

Santa — Neal — gave an encouraging smile that wrinkled his cheeks and then turned away to make the call.

She pursed her lips. What other bad thing could possibly happen now? She'd lost Tanner and gotten stranded in a strange town. *His* hometown.

Seconds later, Neal reappeared. "He'll be here in a minute."

She could only nod. It wasn't that she felt ungrateful. She was just disappointed to have to be grateful again. After this, she would return home, get on her biggest, comfiest pajamas, and watch Netflix. Once the thought came into her head, she wanted that moment with an almost physical longing.

She stood leaning against the Camry until Seth arrived. It was a bold move, since any moment could bring Tanner around the corner, but she felt numb. He hadn't appeared anyway.

Seth roared next to her in a diesel Jeep Cherokee. He looked at her as he parked as though he wanted to say something right away, but couldn't because of the noise. The mechanical scream subsided into silence.

He got out and slammed the door. "You stuck?" he asked.

She mentally filed through about four sarcastic responses before answering, "I just need a jump."

"Not a problem." He hopped back toward his car and opened

the hood. With that same bustling, busy air he'd had in the kitchen, he scurried to retrieve jumper cables from the back seat. The thick, yellow cords were grimy with oil or dirt. "Can you pop your hood?"

"Oh, sure." She pulled the level by the driver's side door and yanked the hood open. She cast a furtive glance down the street. No Tanner.

The operation was finished in sixty seconds. After her car purred to life, Seth petted the Camry as though it were an animal that had been sick. "All set," he said.

"Thank you!" She felt more honest gratitude now than she had even felt at their house.

The car was running. She could finally go home and forget this nightmare ever happened. Visions of ice cream and tea and fuzzy socks and sad Christmas music played through her head as she slid into the driver's seat again. She revved the engine once or twice, just to make sure that the car wouldn't stall. It sounded good.

"Okay!" Seth yelled at her through the closed door. "You be safe!" He gave a cursory wave.

A grim smile crept over her face as she pulled away from the parking spot and started rolling away from Tall Pine. It might be a cute town, but she would never go back there again. Never.

She didn't turn on the radio this time. Silence let her stew in her sadness and feel the numbing beauty of the trees around her. Maybe she should text Tanner and let him know she was alive, at least.

No. He doesn't need to know. Besides, he'd only left one text and one voice message since last night. He must have known he couldn't explain his actions, but it stung that he didn't try harder to win her back. He must be just fine letting her go. After all, he had *Angie.*

She stepped harder on the gas, whirring around the next curve.

The Camry shuddered, jerking her forward. It kept going, but in the feeble kind of way that said it couldn't make it very far. She bit back a curse and looked for a place to pull off. Finally, a patch of dirt appeared around the next bend. Clearly she was not the only one who had to pull off at an odd spot in the mountains.

After the car completely died, she let go of the steering wheel and let her hands hang limp at her sides for a moment. *I should cry, just let it all out.* But her hot eyes had no tears. Something like resignation had replaced her grief. She wasn't sure which was better. This felt just as hopeless.

She pulled out her phone to call someone. She had Tanner's number, and Jesse's. Those were the only two people she knew how to contact within two hundred miles. Would it be so bad to call Jesse and instruct him not to say anything to Tanner? That option felt a little underhanded.

She winced. Did she have to call Tanner? The only other possibility, she thought wildly, was to look up the number for one of the stores on Main Street and ask for Santa.

In desperation, she pulled up Google. *Santa it is.*

Google loaded… and loaded… and loaded…

She waited three full minutes before accepting that there wasn't enough service to use the internet. Still, the phone said she had enough service to make one call.

She bit the back of her lip until blood almost came out. Sucking a breath in through her nose, she punched the button for her contacts. A raised button would have been much more satisfying than a flat phone screen.

Jesse Bingham.

Tanner Bingham.

She hesitated. *It's the least he can do...* She steeled herself and dialed.

BACKUP PLAN

The phone only rang once. "Hello? Lex?" Tanner's voice sounded scared and hopeful. For a second it seemed like she had just imagined his hand on Angie's knee. Why was she running away? She loved that voice.

"I'm stuck on the side of the road," she said, forcing her voice emotionless. "Could you take me to the nearest car repair place?"

"Where are you?"

She looked around, but there were no street signs, just a large cliff of rock broken at the turn-off. "I think I'm about two miles down the mountain." There was only one main way into Tall Pine, so that had to be enough.

"I'll be right there."

He said it so hopefully that she added, "Okay. It's the least you can do." Saying it aloud wasn't as satisfying as saying it in her head.

There was a little silence. "Be there in a minute. Bye, Lex."

Her stomach knotted as she waited for him to arrive. He'd always been a fast driver so he would get here in no time. The snow from the night before hadn't even stuck on the roads.

A familiar dark gray Subaru Impreza pulled up beside her. He slowed to an apologetic speed before pulling on the emergency brake. He always used the emergency brake when he stopped. Maybe the habit was left over from living in a mountain town.

She didn't get out of the car. She knew she should, but she didn't.

Tanner—broad-shouldered, smiling Tanner—walked to her door. She could barely look at him. Summoning courage, she got out of the car, detached, mechanical. "I think it's dead," she said, stepping quickly away from him toward his car.

"Are you sure I can't jump it for you?" he asked.

The suggestion made her irrationally furious. She whirled. "No, you can't jump it for me. It's dead. Just get me somewhere that can fix it." She instantly felt guilty for her tone.

They both got into the Impreza in silence. He shook his head ruefully a few times before starting the car. "I really didn't mean to—"

"Just drive."

"I wasn't planning to meet Angie there last night," he continued.

She scoffed.

"I don't know what I was thinking."

He still hadn't driven onto the road. Lexi felt a rock in the pit of her stomach. Her pain wouldn't let her responses out.

That seemed to be all he could say too, because he finally pulled out on the road.

"Here? Seriously?"

"It's the only place I know of nearby." Tanner's tone had an edge to it. He must have thought that, despite her coldness, she had called him to get back together. As time had gone on and she made no move to do that, his attitude had gotten frostier too.

They were back in Tall Pine.

Her cheeks felt hot as they drove past Santa on Main Street. He didn't notice her in Tanner's car. He was too busy greeting last-minute shoppers on the sidewalk. His black gloves were raised in a happy greeting.

"It's just down here," Tanner said.

A couple blocks down, he turned onto a side street. A fifties-looking sign outside just said CARS. Since there wasn't a nice lot for selling cars, that must mean that he fixed them. At least, she hoped.

Instead of a man, a blonde woman came out. Teeth bared against the sun, she emerged in white coveralls as soon as he parked and pulled the emergency brake.

Lexi hurried to get out first. If Tanner ordered the repair with her standing next to him, she might feel like she owed him something.

"Yes!" she said, as though the woman had already said hello. "Hi, um, my car is stranded a little ways that way." She pointed. "It's a Camry, and I think the battery's dead. There might be something else wrong too."

Tanner turned to her. "I offered to jump it for you," he said in an undertone.

"Somebody else already did this morning."

"Really? Lex, you know you could have—"

"I'll send a tow out there right away," said the blonde woman loudly. Something clanged in the shop behind her. She was probably used to talking over noise. Out here in the stillness, it sounded like she was announcing Lexi's problems to the whole town.

"Thanks," Lexi said, more quietly. She walked closer to the woman. Hopefully Tanner wouldn't follow. "How much is the tow? And the battery. How much would a new battery cost?"

"With installation, the battery will cost you upwards of two hundred." The woman didn't lower her voice.

The pancakes churned inside her at the number. "That's without the tow?"

The woman blinked her squinted eyes a couple times. "Yes. The tow will depend on how far your car is. Can you give me the license plate?"

As Lexi recited numbers and letters, her mind spun. Around and around and around the number two hundred. And car repair places always cost more than expected. What if towing the Camry to the shop cost another hundred?

Before she came, the Binghams had assured her that she would stay at their house, eat their food, open their presents. It was their treat. She took them at their word. But how stupid —how *stupid*—she'd been to leave herself so little wiggle room. If she paid that much for repairs, she wouldn't have enough to get gas for the way home.

But Tanner was standing behind her. He probably had already noticed the way her posture was different or something. He was usually good at reading her. She just hadn't been good at reading him.

She composed her face into a pleasant neutral before turning to face him again. "Looks like everything's under control. I'm sorry to take you away from your family so close to Christmas." The goodbye was implied.

"Look, Lex..."

"I don't want to hear it."

"Don't be like that. I want to explain. Just let me explain!"

She set her jaw firmly. Nothing he could say would make her change her mind. *I've secretly become a doctor and was checking her whole leg for fractures. We were practicing for our high-school play. Angie said she'd kill me if I didn't play along.*

He seemed to be lost for words too. After a second, he cleared his throat. "I don't think you saw..." He tried again. "I want to be with you." He lowered his head, pleading, puppy-eyed.

She laughed humorlessly. "That's not what it looked like to me."

"It was a mistake. It wasn't what it looked like."

"Well, which one? Did you make a mistake or not?"

"I—" His tone got angry. "I made a mistake. Now can we drop it and move on? It's not like we did anything!"

"Okay," Lexi said, revving up. If it had been warmer, she would have rolled up her sleeves. "Here's what I see. I get here early to surprise you. I find you and you're feeling up an old girl-friend that I know, I *know*, left you brokenhearted. You do that when we're serious together. How am I supposed to feel?"

"Honestly, Lex—"

"No." Tears stung her eyes. Anger at what he'd done and anger at having him see her weakness burst out. "No, Tanner. I loved you! And you couldn't even stay faithful to me for five minutes."

That wasn't how she wanted to tell him. She hadn't meant to tell him at all.

His face went still and white. He dropped his eyes.

She wanted to stand there and look at him, to freeze the moment so she could really feel what was happening. But there was no time to think or watch the dark eyelashes hiding his eyes.

"You can go now," she said. "I won't be a backup plan."

SETH

*L*exi thumbed the edge of the smudgy glass.

Everything was smudgy here, even the smoky orange lights. The tables and counter looked a little smudgy as well, but that could have been the whisky shots. She wouldn't have the money to make it back to Columbus anyway, so why not feel better for a little while? Problem was, she didn't feel better. Her head floated above her problems a little, but the bar made her sad. Sitting there alone, she regarded the whole place with melancholy.

The car wouldn't be ready until after Christmas.

She was screwed.

Trapped in a nightmare—isn't that how everyone wants to spend the happiest day of the year? She sucked at the glass, but there was nothing left at the bottom.

"Oh my god." A voice from behind her.

She spun around. Who was that? He looked a little familiar. Sandy hair, dusty skin, busy expression. He wore jeans and a green jacket with a high collar. His eyes were large as he looked at her, eyebrows arched high, almost into his hairline. Seth. That was his name.

"Lexi?" he said.

"Yeah?"

"What are you doing here? I thought you had to get home."

"I do have to get home." She said it without slurring, but it took extra concentration.

"You're not driving home like this," he said.

"I can do what I want," she answered petulantly, looking back at the glass.

"No." He came up quickly and sat beside her. Cold air from outside radiated from his jacket. "I mean, you just can't drive. Give me your keys."

She scrunched up her forehead and hugged her purse. "No."

"Give me your keys."

Why was he so pushy? "No!"

"Then just tell me you won't drive like this."

"I can't!" she said miserably. "Car's in the shop. I'm *stuck* here."

His intensity melted a little. Seth's gaze moved to the empty glass she was holding. "I'm sorry."

She waggled her head in agreement.

He paused a little longer than most people did in the middle of a conversation. The look on his face meant he was considering something, or wrestling with himself. "Here, let me get that." He shoved his hand in his pocket and brought out a credit card. "Marla," he called to the same bartender who had helped Angie when she was here yesterday.

Marla came over, this time dressed in an ugly Christmas sweater and jean overalls. "Here for the pickup?" she asked.

"Yeah." He tossed his card. "Just add her bill to mine."

"Having a party?" Lexi asked, a little too sad and a little too drunk to protest.

"Work party," he replied. Then he sighed. "Do you have a place to stay tonight?"

She pursed her lips far out as though she had to think about it. "Nah."

"Then you can stay with us again until your car is fixed."

"Don't you have a work party?"

"I'll get there late. Let me just take you home." He faltered. "Not like…!"

She waved one hand at him. She knew what he meant. "I'm a strong woman, you know," she said. "I was here to see my boyfriend. Cause I lov—I loved him, and his family's here. But then there was this *girl*. This other girl, she sat right there." She pointed at the hateful seat.

"I'm really sorry," said Seth, and he seemed to mean it. "I didn't know."

"You didn't ask," she said loftily. "You were too busy to look at me." This dangerous level of openness was as heady as another drink. Why shouldn't she just spill the truth?

"I didn't expect you to be there," he said. "I'm sorry. It's a weird time for me and my dad."

"It's weird?" she asked, catching the word. "Your dad is Santa."

He laughed. He had a nice smile, big and dimpled like his dad's. "Yeah, he's done that for years."

"Here are those growlers," Marla announced, setting four of them on the counter between them.

"Best beer in town," Seth told Lexi.

"Only beer in town," she replied moodily.

"Okay, let's get you home," he said, paying Marla and pulling Lexi to her feet.

*I*t must have been a few hours later when Seth came back home after his work party.

He had dropped Lexi off at Santa's house—Santa was working a late shift—and told her to make herself at home. After rifling aimlessly through the cupboards for a few minutes, she'd found an old sleeve of Girl Scout cookies and settled herself in front of the TV. It didn't take long to find the Hallmark Christmas movie marathon. Between Halloween and New Year's, they played all their hundreds of Christmas romances in a row. She knew they were cheesy. She knew men like that didn't exist, that sudden proposals were a bad life decision, but she didn't care. She ate them up with all the fervor of a puppy with a whipped cream can.

She was in the middle of her second movie when Seth returned. He flipped the switch on, drowning out the bluish glow of the TV in the darkness. She groaned and pulled the blanket closer to her face. Stacey, the big gray dog, jumped from where she had been lying at Lexi's feet to wiggle and wag and greet Seth. The Girl Scout cookie sleeve, now empty, softly crinkled as it fell to the floor.

"I thought you'd be asleep," Seth said, drawing off his gray scarf with one hand and petting Stacey's ears with the other.

"Just one more," Lexi replied. She meant the Hallmark movie.

He came over and looked at the television like an old man would. "Isn't that just going to make you sad?"

She paused the movie. "I like them."

To her surprise, he plopped down on the couch next to her. He smelled like pine candles and cranberry cocktails. She shied a few millimeters away.

"So what is this?' he asked.

"You don't have to…" Her voice dwindled as she ran out of energy to protest. Seth didn't strike her as the kind of guy who would watch Hallmark movies at—she twisted to see the clock on the microwave behind her—12:49 AM.

He grabbed the remote and pushed play.

"See, I don't get that," he said almost immediately. "Why do all these people get Christmas trees on Christmas Eve?" He wrestled his way out of his long blue jacket and hopped up to hang it on the peg by the door with his scarf. He flicked off the light again. So he did intend to watch this movie with her. "Do they buy an expensive tree just to look at it for forty-eight hours? That seems like a waste."

She took the remote back and paused the movie. He couldn't talk through the whole thing.

"Nobody does that in real life," he complained in a comfortable tone that suggested that they'd been friends for years. Maybe he'd been drinking too.

"It's the *feeling* you get on Christmas Eve," she explained. "Like the best reality's all squished together." She balled her hands into one fist to demonstrate.

He looked at her hands and made a good-natured face.

After a pause, she said, "So, work party? What do you do?" She might as well be pleasant if he was going to stay.

His motions as he stretched on the couch had the slightly sloppy quality of someone who had just enjoyed a party. "I'm an attorney."

Oh my goodness! This is nothing like a Hallmark movie. Losing a carpenter and stuck with an attorney...

"So, you're on the phone a lot, I bet," she said.

"Pretty often," he agreed, not self-conscious about matching the negative trope. "There aren't many of us, so I stay busy." He smiled at her, loosened up by the beer.

"It was a small party, then?" She had pictured one of those large ordeals they always showed in chick flicks. Huge, impeccably decorated warehouses, flowing champagne, flowing smiles, everyone handsome or beautiful... Did any Christmas party actually look like that?

"Well, yeah," he said. "We met at my boss's house. Only two people besides me regularly work at the office, so they were there with their families. We had a good time." He ran a thumb and forefinger meditatively over the dusty five o' clock shadow below his chin. "Are we turning the movie back on?"

She caught the plural *we*. "I was going to finish it and then go to bed," she said, giving him an out if he wanted one. She would be all right on her own. His presence always felt hurried, as though she should be doing something else too. Part of her wanted to stew alone anyway.

"Mm kay." He leaned back, releasing some of that busy energy.

Resigned to his company, she drew her knees up to her chest under the blanket, getting as comfortable as possible, and pressed play.

In a second, she stopped it again. "You don't have a Christmas tree here, do you?" She couldn't remember seeing one. Squinting into the darkness didn't reveal a tree in any hidden corners of the living room. The matter seemed urgent.

"No," he replied, not looking at her. "We haven't had one for a few years. It's fine."

"Your dad is literally *Santa*. You need a tree." She let her legs down off the couch again and twisted to face him.

He turned his head. The garish TV light reflected off his high cheekbones. His eyes had sobered to a dull sheen. "He doesn't want one."

"That's ridiculous."

"It's no big deal."

"You don't even have a fake one somewhere?"

"No. We stopped putting them up when my mom passed away."

She quieted. "Oh. I'm so sorry."

"Three years ago. Car accident," he explained.

"Oh," she said again. "A tree wouldn't cheer you up?"

"Would it cheer you up?" It was a real question, not an accusation.

"Maybe," she sang, treading carefully. Though it wasn't much, teasing him was the most fun she'd had in the past twenty-four hours. Of course, she didn't want to hurt him or bring up painful memories.

"You said you're stuck until after Christmas?"

"The twenty-sixth."

"Sucks."

"You think?"

The next silence was so long that she reached for the remote again. Before she pushed the button, the door opened. Neal was home in complete Santa garb.

Seeing him made her think of staying up late on Christmas Eve with her sister. She was five and Jessica was seven. They were breathless and giggly, waiting for Santa to arrive. This was the closest thing to that she'd felt in a long time. A moment of magic.

"Hey, Dad," Seth said, breaking the spell. Stacey's nails scraped in her haste to reach the door.

Neal turned and saw Lexi sitting on the couch. "Oh! Hope I'm not interrupting. Well, I thought you'd gone home!"

"I tried," she replied. "Car broke down, so I'm stuck until after Christmas." Suddenly self-conscious, she realized how presumptuous it was of her to assume they'd let her stay that long. She wasn't sure what to say.

"Ah," Neal said around his beard. He rolled the syllable around as though he were thinking, but it still sounded kind.

"She wants to get a Christmas tree tomorrow," Seth put in.

She made a strangled noise and almost lunged at Seth. She would have smacked him if she'd known him better. What a thing to say!

"It's Christmas Eve," Neal said, his logic matching his son's. You don't get a tree on Christmas Eve.

And who would pay for it? Lexi? She was all but broke, especially now, with the car.

Seth waggled his head to the side in a kind of shrug. "It might be a fun thing to do."

Neal pursed his lips. His mustache bristled. Before answering, he passed through the room, presumably toward his own. "If you want to get a tree, I won't stop you." His tone didn't sound injured or sad, but his wording was carefully chosen.

"All right, we'll go in the morning," Seth said.

"It is morning!" Santa cried as he disappeared into the other room.

TREE ON CHRISTMAS EVE

*L*exi called her mom the next day. They talked for two hours about the breakup before she and Seth went to the Christmas tree lot the next town over. Tall Pine ought to have had its own lot, but they had to go to Kettle, ten minutes away, instead.

Tanner's absence hurt in a lot of little ways. It made her feel smaller. Less wanted. Too many things reminded her of him: a suit in a shop window (he hated wearing suits), kitschy magnets with bears on them (she always thought of him when she saw Colorado-themed merchandise), Seth using the emergency brake.

She suspected that Seth took them both to the lot because he needed something to do with his few days off. It was just as well. She needed something to do too. Without Seth's suggestion, she probably would have wandered around the town feeling sorry for herself.

Seth grabbed a skinny tree by the middle and shook it a little. It wobbled like pencils did when Lexi's friends in junior high held them just right. "These are pretty sad," he said.

She gazed around the lot. Most of the trees were skinny

rejects from the season. That, or they had some kind of deformity. A few of the bushy-looking ones had huge gaps on one side. Half a tree, really. None of them even looked very friendly, like Charlie Brown's Christmas tree.

She tucked a stray piece of hair into her knit cap. "They are," she agreed.

"Do you still want to get one?"

She lifted her chin in a desperate kind of hopefulness. "I think it's the principle of the thing. Ouch!" She had accidentally backed into a larger, lopsided tree. Its sharp needles poked right through her sweater. She spun around and glared at it. The top bent downward, almost as though it had intentionally attacked her.

Seth waved her forward, away from the malicious tree. "I don't think there's a principle here, but maybe we can find a tree that isn't hideous."

"Do you think your dad really won't mind if we bring one home?"

"No, not really. Unless it looks like it lost a fight with other trees."

She couldn't completely stifle a giggle.

Seth had already started eying a new prospect with the seriousness of a critic scrutinizing a piece of art. It had poky branches sticking out like the arms of a T-rex. Still, Seth squinted at it. Was he mocking her? Was he serious? He crossed his arms.

Why do you live with your dad? she thought. It seemed like an insensitive question. Tons of people live with their parents. A busy attorney ought to have enough money to move if he wanted to, though. A loose collection of half-read articles about millennials shuffled through her mind.

He grimaced. "This one is..." He couldn't find the word, apparently, because he just jabbed at it with a finger.

"Can I help you folks out?"

Lexi froze. She knew that voice. It sounded like a slightly

higher, slightly distorted version of a voice she knew very, very well.

Appearing at the end of the aisle of trees came Jesse, Tanner's brother. He wore a button-up flannel, slightly scuffed jeans, tennis shoes, and a name tag. His brown hair was the same shade as his brother's.

Maybe he wouldn't recognize her. They'd only met in person once.

"Lexi? Oh man! What are you doing here?" His tone was an odd mix of glee, accusation, sadness, and confusion. He half-jogged the last few steps toward them. His Tanner-like eyes took in Seth beside her. "Seth, you're here too." It was a question, but he didn't raise the last syllable, as though he didn't want to admit it.

"Hey," Lexi said lamely.

"You know her?" Seth asked, beaming at Jesse.

"You know him?" Lexi shot back furtively.

"Yeah," said Jesse slowly.

None of them moved to leave.

"So, ah, you work here?" Lexi asked.

Jesse shifted his weight to his other foot. "Part time. I need to make some money for college."

"Because you're going next year. Wow, that's coming up soon," she said. It struck her that a full-time Christmas tree lot employee probably wasn't a thing.

"I can't believe it. You're almost done with high school." Seth spoke almost as an older brother would. Almost as Tanner would. She furrowed her brows as she looked at him. How did they know each other?

"Yeah," Jesse said, dusting the full length of his sleeves as though they were covered with snow or dirt. They weren't. A private smile crept onto his face despite the awkwardness. "Yeah, I'm almost done."

"Where are you thinking of going to college?"

"I'm looking at CSU for now."

The boys chatted on, acting completely unaware that Lexi had just broken off a serious relationship with Jesse's brother, broken off her plans to stay with the Binghams, and now was Christmas tree shopping with a different young man rather than leaving town.

A jab in her stomach reminded her that all this information was inevitably getting back to Tanner. At least he knew her car had broken down and wouldn't necessarily assume that she had a secret family with Seth.

"Well, if you folks don't need any more help…" Jesse started to walk away.

You folks. Tanner talked that way, but she hadn't noticed all the residents of Tall Pine using the same downhome expression. It made her think of cowboy hats and preachers.

"Bye!" Seth waved and turned to contemplate more trees.

"What was that?" she hissed as soon as Jesse was out of earshot.

Seth pulled up his lip in a distasteful grimace, as though she'd said something nasty. "What was *what*?"

"How do you know him?"

"I've helped his family out of some legal trouble a couple times. Can't give you the details."

Lexi squinted. "Legal trouble."

"You're not even from here. How do you—?" But he cut himself off. He knew the answer.

"His older brother," Lexi admitted.

"Tanner?"

The word burned. She nodded dejectedly. Hot, sudden tears sprang to her eyes. She didn't want to cry.

"No, hey," said Seth, giving her a side hug. "He's… he's no good. No good for you, probably. I'm sure you did the right thing." His brisk manner reminded her of the distracted pancakes. "How about this one?" He steered her toward a particularly hideous tree, thin, barren, and already crispy.

"That'll go up like a torch," she said.

He laughed. "We'll just be very careful."

GINGER ANN

*L*exi and Seth stepped back. The tree looked crooked.

It shouldn't have come as a surprise. It looked crooked in the lot. And scraggly. A third of it was bald patches and the rest was skinny branches that left no secrets about the trunk inside. The needles were even tinged a little brown. This tree might have been a leftover from last year.

Part of her wanted to attach a heavy round ornament to the top and watch it droop like Charlie Brown's. The other part of her wanted to throw it in the trash.

"Well," Seth began optimistically. His mouth moved with other words, but none came out. He just ended up laughing.

This backlit monstrosity had probably doomed the house forever. They'd never buy a Christmas tree again. Santa would just have to go treeless.

She winced and turned to Seth as he continued to giggle silently. "I don't suppose you have ornaments, do you?" she asked.

He burst out audibly.

"We didn't even think of it," she lamented. The tree had been expensive enough, but now that they had no decorations, she almost felt ashamed of suggesting they go at all.

"That's the ugliest thing I've ever seen," he said.

She let out a breath, thinking of Christmas cards with hopeful jalopies on them, with huge fluffy trees tethered to the top. "It's horrifying," she agreed.

"Well, if we get bed bugs, I'll know who to thank."

She groaned.

"Don't worry, don't worry," he said, bumping his shoulder against hers. "It could be Stacey, who knows." At the sound of her name, the dog scuffled over to sit under Seth's hand. He scratched the top of her head and flopped her ears. "I won't accuse you of anything without hard proof."

She reached out and touched a feeble cluster of pine needles. Two fell off. She looked woefully at Seth. "Very lawyerly of you. So you know the Binghams?"

"A little. Nice family. Sort of." He shot her a look and turned toward the kitchen for a drink of water.

He always seemed to be going somewhere. Why couldn't he stand still for a minute?

"Wait!" she called. "You can't talk about the cases?"

"Confidentiality." He held up a second glass in a question.

She nodded. "Is that really so binding that you can't talk about it?"

"Yep." He handed her the water. "Why are you so interested? Are you thinking of getting back together with Tanner?" He headed for the couch.

"No," she said quickly, and then reconsidered. "No. I won't get back together with him."

"You should have somebody better, anyway."

She made a noncommittal noise. That would be great, but the great ones either didn't notice or only stopped to browse before moving on. "I don't know that there is anybody."

"Well, that's not true." The way he said it reminded her that he was Santa's son. His intonation was like a kindly old man.

"It might be!" she insisted, sitting beside him.

He took a drink of water, eying her over the rim of the glass. "That's ridiculous," he finally said.

"Nobody tends to want me enough." The outburst had come from deep inside her. And she hadn't even been drinking. She blushed. Why was she confiding in Seth, a man she'd just met?

Meditatively, he set his glass on the side table. His look suggested that he might ask to take her hands for some kind of therapeutic exercise. She recoiled. He looked at her with utmost seriousness. "Lexi, we chose that stupid tree. There's always hope for you."

Despite herself, she laughed. "Are you comparing me to Arnold?"

"Arnold?" He looked bewildered.

"What I've decided to call the tree."

"So, it's like our child?"

"Mm hm."

"I feel like I'm back in high school." He grinned and leaned back, running a hand through his dirty blond hair. "Arnold? Are you sure?"

"It's set in stone. Sorry." She felt the tension creep at the far edges of the room. "What would you have chosen?" she asked. Seth was a good person to tease. He wanted to do, to fix, to move, so he would go along with her bits or else get turned around by her hypotheticals.

He considered. "Ginger Ann."

"Are you serious? Like Ginger Ale."

"Oh no." He raised his eyebrows in mock solemnity. "Don't mock our little girl."

"Our little girl is missing a few arms," she said.

"Pshaw! She has at least two. That's all a person needs." He arched backward toward the backlit tree. Though he strained the muscles in his arms, he couldn't quite touch Ginger's spindly branches. His fingers waved uselessly in the air.

"Do you and Ginger have holiday plans today?" she asked. It had to be four o' clock.

"Not really."

"What is it with you? It's like you don't celebrate Christmas." She ticked off the offenses with her fingers. "No tree, no decorations of any kind, no plans on Christmas Eve…"

He watched her with a little smirk on his face. He had surprisingly nice eyes in this light. Something in her sank. She shook off the notion and looked away from his warm, inviting gaze. He wasn't being forward. Maybe he didn't even notice he was looking at her that way. Maybe he looked at Stacey like that when she did something cute.

He sat in the moment a little longer, as though he expected her list to go on. "I must be a Christmas failure," he said.

"No," she said, too quickly.

He smiled. "Do you want to do something together then?"

She smiled back.

❄

"I feel ridiculous."

"Probably because you're wearing light-up reindeer antlers." Seth flicked them and a tiny bell jingled.

"We're so lame," Lexi said. "There has to be something better than this to do on Christmas Eve." But she was smiling.

"We're both fried," he agreed.

Lexi considered a wall of cheap, shiny earrings. Florescent light made them sparkle yellow and blue. "Jingle Bell Rock" sang merrily above them.

It was a melancholy kind of happiness, a little tainted by Tanner's absence and the fact that she couldn't be with her family today. She glanced at Seth, who regarded a tower of Santa and elf hats with an empty stare. He was better company than she would have thought. Spending the day with him had almost made her forget what a crummy day she should have been having.

"You have to try an elf one," she said, grabbing one from the stand.

He backed up. "No no no."

She reached up toward his head. The green hat might not even fit. It looked like it was made for a child.

"No no!" he repeated, and then he lowered his voice. "Lexi, no. I already have one of those."

Now it was her turn to fall back. "Seriously? You own an elf hat?"

He looked at her meaningfully.

"A whole costume?" She laughed at the image. Her first thought was the getup Will Ferrell wore in *Elf*: the pointy hat crushing Seth's dirty blond hair, yellow tights, huge curly-toed shoes, the felt-looking green jerkin. Seth wasn't as smiley as Buddy, but his sudden grins burst like joyful fireworks. Seth had the nervous energy of an elf. Maybe the outfit would suit him after all. His personality did lie somewhere between an elf and a lawyer. Well, most people's did. Those were on pretty far ends of the spectrum.

"My dad made me help him out sometimes when I was in high school," he explained.

"Do you still have it?"

He flattened his mouth and turned to a display of Lip Smackers.

"You do!" she cried.

"No!" he protested, and groaned. "I should have burned it years ago." His woebegone expression made her smile.

Faint green and red lights alternated across his forehead. She took off the blinking reindeer headband.

Pointing at her, he said, "You're not seeing it." There was a bit of a laugh in the gesture.

"Let's go," she said, giggling.

It wasn't snowing outside, but it was cold, freeze you in your tracks when the wind blows kind of cold. She dug a hat out of her purse and jammed it over her ears. Despite the frigid wind and icy sidewalks, many people strolled along the street doing last-minute shopping. A lot of them were tourists, judging from the sweatshirts some wore. "A Colorado Christmas," one said above a cartoon moose that sat looking confused yet peaceful as tinsel and ornaments hung from its huge antlers.

The ground slid.

Her right leg shot forward on nothing as she jack-knifed back.

Strong hands grabbed her bicep hard enough to stop her just before she hit the ground. She glided her foot back under her. The sudden jerk made the back of her neck feel a little out of alignment.

"You okay?" Seth asked.

"Yeah."

When she stood back on her own two legs, he let go. She gingerly took a step, body braced in case she hit black ice again.

Seth offered his arm.

"I'll just take you down too," she said. "But maybe your shoes have more tread. Women's shoes are the worst." She wore boots, but even those had only a whisper of tread on them.

"I think we'll be fine," he said.

She wrapped her hands around his jacketed arm. He felt sturdy, so she instantly felt more confident to walk forward.

Until she almost ran over a little girl.

GINGERBREAD HOUSE

"*W*ould you like to buy a gingerbread house?" she called, her black curls shaking adorably. She had to be only five and six.

"A gingerbread house?" Seth echoed, his grin mirroring her excitement.

"Yeah, they're only fifteen dollars. We're raising money for field trips!"

"Can we see one of these gingerbread houses?" he asked.

The girl all but pulled him over to a table tucked just inside a clothing store. A woman, presumably the girl's mother—same cherubic cheeks and dark curly hair—sat behind it. She had a bright smile with just a hint of exhaustion.

On the table were flat boxes with pictures of a grand gingerbread house on each one.

Lexi's heart sank a little as her vision of fully formed sugar cottages was flattened.

Her side buzzed. Seth abruptly extricated his arm from hers and reached into his coat pocket for his phone. She'd forgotten she was still hanging onto him. No need inside. But it was nice to have companionship, especially when everything was so warm and gold, glittering with holiday spirit.

"Give me a sec," he said, and answered the phone. "Hello, Seth Aldridge…"

Lexi turned awkwardly to the girl and her mother. *She wouldn't pay fifteen dollars for a flat gingerbread house, but she tried to smile anyway.* "So, tell me how this works."

The girl jumped forward, thrilled to give her prepared speech. "The gingerbread"—she caught her breath and started again —"the gingerbread mix is inside. You make the mix, and then put it in the molds. The molds are all the walls and stuff. Then you use the icing to glue it together!"

She was so proud, standing there in her red and white velvet jacket. But that sounded like a lot of work. For fifteen dollars, she wanted the walls made already, at least.

"Oh," Lexi replied. "That sounds fun."

The mother must have caught a note in her voice because she gave a forgiving smile. *It's all right if you walk away,* it seemed to say.

"I don't know," Lexi said. "I need to think about it."

She stepped back and grabbed her phone from her purse. Practically hiding behind a rack of fleece pullovers, she realized that the hat made her head too warm in this heated store.

The time glowed 6:51 on the front of the touchscreen. Four text messages. One phone message.

Mom: *I hope you're having a magical Christmas Eve. We're thinking about you. Say thank you to Santa & son for us. xo*

Tanner: *Did u ever get ur car fixed? U can still stay with us. worried about u*

Tanner: *ru there?*

Jessica: *Hey funkopop wheres that sweater you wore to the ugly sweater party last year?*

She responded to her family, but left Tanner's text and

message unanswered. What could he say that wasn't obvious already?

A few minutes later, Seth reappeared. "There you are. I got us a gingerbread house." He said it as though it were something mundane and necessary, like a pair of socks.

Gladness bloomed in her chest for the little girl and her mother. "Who was that on the phone?"

"Client," he said, heading for the door. As he opened it, he offered her his arm again, the one not holding a labor-intensive Christmas project. She took it.

A few minutes of walking under white Christmas lights, and then, "You're awfully quiet. We should get home and make this." He shook the box. "You were the one saying we didn't have enough Christmas cheer."

"It's a lot of work."

He pitched his voice high. "You don't have a *Christmas tree?* How horrible!"

"Stop it!" She hip-checked him.

He smiled afterward, looking at the ground. He had such a nice smile, straight teeth, wide dimples, happiness without a tinge of self-consciousness or irony. It was the kind of smile that drew you into its private world.

She drew up short. *Why am I thinking things like that?*

It didn't take long to get back to the Santa family's small house. She hung onto Seth's strong arm the whole way because of the black ice. But this time she paid attention to the kindness and to the muscles underneath.

Once on the dark porch, she let go. The right side of her body went cold with the wind. She shivered, dancing on her toes and hugging herself. Seth drew out a key and let them into the house.

She barreled inside. A scrabbling of nails on hardwood and the dog barreled into her on the way to Seth. He bent down to pet her ears. Arnold (or Ginger Ann) was just a spindly silhouette against the front window.

"I'll turn the oven on," Seth announced, shrugging off his coat and hanging on the peg across from the door.

"Is your dad working again tonight?"

"Christmas Eve," he said, by way of explanation. He passed her on the way to the little kitchen and gave her the gingerbread kit. "Can you see what we need?"

She read the ingredients they needed to add to the mix. Pretty simple. They probably had everything in the fridge already. Together they drew out the ingredients and a bowl. The mix took three minutes to put together. They worked hurriedly in silence.

"I feel like we need Christmas music," Lexi finally said.

He eyed her. "Still not Christmasy enough?"

"It's Christmas Eve!" On Christmas Eve, her family always ate Christmas cookies, opened presents, went to church, and drove together through neighborhoods with the craziest light displays. At least they needed Christmas music.

"Then put some on." Seth stirred the mix vigorously while she chose a Nat King Cole album on her phone. The opening notes of "The First Noel" made her insides long for childhood with her family, to be surrounded by people that she loved. "That sounds like a good one," he said.

"Yeah," she replied, pulling the house molds from the box. The sound made Stacey look up sharply, wide eyes obviously expecting a treat. Wasn't sugar poisonous to dogs or something? She couldn't remember, and wouldn't risk it.

Seth stopped mixing and looked at the little wall-shaped template. After a second, he pushed up his sleeves. The oven warmed up the kitchen as a fireplace would. "Those don't look like the ones I've done before."

"You've made gingerbread houses like this?"

"Well, not like this." He paused, cleaning his teeth with his tongue as he looked for the right words. "My mom and I used to make gingerbread from scratch. Not every year, but most years."

She laughed nervously. "So this is different, huh?"

"Yeah. She loved Christmas." He dropped the spoon in the bowl. "She… this is the third anniversary."

This felt too private to share with her, a relative stranger. Why was he sharing this intimate knowledge? "I didn't know."

He stirred like someone waking up. "You couldn't have known," he said quickly. "I'm glad you're here, actually. I hated it when my boss gave me a few days off for Christmas. I just wanted to work through it, you know? Dad could work, but they made me go home."

"I bet your dad is glad that you're here too."

"Yes, he is." He spoke, hesitating in odd places. "I knew he wouldn't be all right for a while, so I've stayed here. I don't mind." He picked up the flimsy mold. "My mom would be appalled!" he laughed.

When the tension broke, she laughed too. "Maybe the house will turn out all right," she said. "Let's get it in the oven."

They stuck it in, molds clattering on the metal shelf and set a timer. Nat King Cole cheerfully sang "Deck the Hall." Seth's smile had faded, replaced by introspective blankness. Mechanically, he grabbed the dirty bowl and spoon and washed them in the sink. He almost collided with her to grab the dish towel to dry them off. She hated to see him sad, but it was his right to mourn if he wanted to. His mood affected hers, though, and made her consider her own melancholy thoughts. The smooth music only amplified them. She had to make a change.

"Okay," she said, all business. "What now?"

"I could get you your present."

That was unexpected. "What?"

"Or do you open presents on Christmas Day?"

"What? You got me something?"

"Well, yeah."

"I didn't get you anything."

He waved her away. "That's fine. You're the one who can't spend Christmas with your family. I didn't wrap it or anything."

Her stomach fell pleasantly. A smile tugged at her mouth. "Okay. Is it your elf costume?"

He groaned and rolled his eyes. "You're never seeing that."

"That's what you said. But a girl can hope." She stilled. That last bit sounded like flirting. It *was* flirting. She was flirting with Seth. Well, was that so bad? She was single now, and he had been kinder to her than almost anyone else she knew.

He gave a closed-lipped smile, all dimples, and went back to the front door. He pulled something out of his coat pocket. "It's not that big a deal," he said, handing it to her. "Merry Christmas."

It was a pair of delicately flat gold earrings shaped like bells. Her insides felt warm. "Thank you." She opened her arms, paused. "Can I?"

He met her hug halfway.

"Thank you," she repeated. "You know, you've cheered me up on a couple of really bad days. What can I do to cheer you up?" She looked up at him sideways as she pulled out her hoop earrings.

The music changed. Instead of Nat King Cole, Christina Aguilera started singing about Christmastime. Seth cocked his head as he looked down at her, a teasing look in his eyes.

"Yeah, so I sometimes listen to Christina," she said, putting in her new earrings. "What do you think?" She felt the edges of them with her fingertips.

"I think they look good," he said.

The beat of the music suddenly made her rock with it, tipping her shoulders back and forth. Returning his teasing gaze, and upping it to a dare, she started swaying more vigorously.

He smiled but didn't dance.

"Come on!" she said.

He paused for a second, considering. Puckering his lips, he relented and snaked his neck to the beat.

She laughed as they started dancing around each other like

drunken puffins. Neither of them had great timing or fancy foot-work. What they did have was a blast.

The next upbeat song started. For a second, she thought he might stop, but he took her hand and twirled her right back into their awkward dance. She mouthed the words with all the vigor of a contestant in a lip sync competition. He didn't know the words, or wouldn't admit to knowing them, so he just watched and danced along, handing her various things for mics.

She pretended to sing the last impressive Christina run when the timer beeped.

Still feeling silly and a little out of breath, she rushed on her toes to the oven. "Mitts, please." She set down the potato masher she'd been singing into and pinched her fingers like a crab.

The mitts appeared in her hands.

The gingerbread walls and roof looked a little crispy but solid. It felt like time for another change of music. Pentatonix.

She gently wrestled the gingerbread out of its mold and Seth kneaded the stale white icing.

"I think Arnold is going to love it," she said, easing the last part of the tiny roof onto a cooling rack.

"That's not the name," he said. "What did I call it?"

She hesitated as though she had to think about it. "Ginger Ann."

"Her name's Ginger Ann."

"Ginger Ann? Gingerbread? It's too much ginger."

"No such thing."

"Is the icing ready?"

"Just about."

After a trying minute, they realized that they had to cut off the tip of the icing container before anything would come out.

Seth drew a shakily straight line of icing on the plastic stand. Lexi pressed the first wall into it. When she let go, it immediately slumped over. She put it back upright and held it. Same with the second wall. Hopefully the icing between the two adjacent walls would help so she wouldn't have to keep standing here, holding up two walls of the gingerbread house. Seth carefully glued between the walls. After about a minute, she let go again. More slowly this time, the walls fell to opposite sides.

"You'll have to hold the other ones," she said.

He didn't look at her, too intent on making his frosting line. "Just hold both with one hand."

"So I get *all* of them?"

His eyebrow rose. He glanced at her. "We can take turns if you want."

"That's okay. I can take all of them."

The four walls went up slowly. She held them all in place. "The roof is going to take forever to stick."

"Patience," he said in some kind of accent that made her think it was a reference to a movie, but she couldn't remember which one it was.

"Yes, your favorite thing," she said, hunched over the roofless house.

"I think it's probably ready now."

Lexi doubted it. The walls felt like they would slide on the wet icing. To prove her theory, she gently lifted up her fingers until only the slightest pressure remained. Her hands looked like dancers on top of the walls. She lifted them away.

Success!

But then, one wall started caving inward. She swiftly reached out to stop it from falling. So did Seth. Their fingers touched. It felt different than when he had grabbed her hand dancing a moment ago. Both of them noticed the touch this time. Warm, rough fingers against hers.

She placed the wall back up where it belonged. Seth pulled away and said, "Here." From a drawer he pulled out some utensil that he lay across the top of the weakest walls. The house stood unmoving.

She didn't want to look at him. That would just be an admission of the electricity she'd felt. He'd be able to see it in her eyes. She cleared her throat, trying to think of something useful to do. "Won't be able to put the roof on for a while," she said, and glanced at the glaring microwave clock. Almost ten o' clock. They hadn't turned on many lights.

"Well, we can't stop now. Ginger Ann and a half-built gingerbread house? You're trying to cheer me up, right?"

"Yeah." The word came out dejected. Something deep inside her welled up, as it had years ago. It didn't matter that she started to feel a new spark, hope that grew tentatively again. If anything, she was always a stepping stone, not a destination. *Not enough. You're a diversion, a stop to the right one. You're never the right one.* This hope was false hope. Better not to get hurt again.

"Hey." He bent down to her line of sight. "What's wrong?"

"Nothing."

"Tanner really did a number on you, didn't he?"

"What, no! I mean, well… yeah, he did."

"He can be an idiot, sometimes."

She rolled her eyes. "I know."

"No. I've known him since he was a kid. He doesn't know a good thing when he has it."

Something about his tone of voice made her stomach hollow. Was he calling her a good thing? Did it matter? "That's nice of you to say."

When she didn't offer more, he sighed. His hands moved as though they longed to have something to do. "How long do you think this house'll take to dry?"

"A million years?" she suggested.

"Maybe half an hour? That seems more than reasonable." The ease with which he used the phrase made her think he must use all the time as a lawyer.

They'd both lost some of the energy they'd had when they danced around like happy fools, so they headed naturally toward the couch. Stacey followed them and lay against it.

Lexi snuggled into a blanket. "Do you want to watch another—?"

"God no."

"You watched it with me last time."

"I was under the influence."

"I'm sure there are, like, ten on TV right now."

"There are also infomercials. We could learn about ten ladders in one."

She primly tucked the blanket in around her. "We don't have to watch anything. It's only half an hour. We can wait it out." They waited for a moment in silence. "I think Arnold wants to," she said, and dove for the remote.

Desperately, Seth grabbed it at the same time. He pried her fingers off the end and held it back over his head, triumphant.

She was short but they were sitting—equal ground. Going for it again, she reached past him. When that didn't work, she pulled on his arm to bring it closer. With her whole weight on his arm, he had no choice but to bend it. She felt the remote's hard shell and soft plastic buttons but couldn't get a good grip. One at a time, she pulled his fingers. He loosened his grip, but she couldn't take the remote at the same time. Finally, it clattered to the floor.

She realized she was laughing, and he was laughing. She was sprawled on top of him.

Neither moved to get up.

Her insides dropped.

He was warm and sturdy beneath her, and he looked at her. Heat rushed to her cheeks. His laugh faded naturally away as his gaze trailed from her eyes to her forehead to her lips. He raised one hand carefully and traced her jawline with a finger, like a question. *Is this okay?* His touch sent a thrill through her. Though her heart pounded so hard she knew he could feel it, she didn't move away.

Slowly, he cupped her face with one hand and felt her pierced ear, the fingers trailing to the edges of the golden bells. His smiled breath warmed her mouth.

The door opened.

Seth and Lexi jumped apart as though they'd had an electric shock. Neal was home. Santa on Christmas Eve.

She jumped to her feet and said, "I think we can put the roof on now." Her voice sounded too loud. Had she been whispering?

Stacey let out a small bark as she leapt to her feet, wagging at Neal.

Seth got up too and got the icing ready. When Neal came around to look at what they were talking about, his eyes twinkled like the real St. Nick. There was truth in those eyes. Maybe he knew everything. Just in case, they'd pretend like they weren't about to kiss. Lexi could hardly believe it herself.

Seth touched the four walls. They held firm. It had somehow been half an hour. "You're right. Looks ready."

"Ho ho ho!" That couldn't have been Neal's real laugh. His Santa persona had probably just been on for too long. "Is that a gingerbread house?" he asked.

It was small. It had no roof. But yes, it was supposed to be a gingerbread house. "There was a fundraiser," Lexi began.

"A little girl was selling them. So cute. So we had to try it out," Seth finished.

Surely Neal could tell that something was up from the breathlessness in their voices, but he didn't press them. He just hummed in that comfortable, grandfatherly way. Stroking his beard, he gave the tiny walls one last glance, and then looked up at his son. "Well, it's late," he said. "I'm going to get some sleep."

Seth held up a hand, put it down. Was he going to protest? Did he already regret being alone with her? "Okay," he said. "Good night."

"Merry Christmas!" Neal replied with all the gusto and flourish of Santa himself. The sound warmed her.

Once Neal's velvet suit had disappeared into the house, the sound of Michael Bublé singing about coming home for Christmas filtered back into her consciousness. Seth stood awkwardly holding the frosting bag. He didn't move. There was a question in his eyes.

She didn't answer it. "Let's put the roof on," she said.

RUDE AWAKENING

$\mathscr{A}$ loud noise woke Lexi the next morning. She sat straight up in bed, clutching the Thomas the Tank Engine comforter. It didn't sound like clashing dishes making room for pancakes. The sound came again.

An angry knock at the door.

Who would come to anyone's house on Christmas—*Christmas* —and be that angry? The pounding didn't stop. It just paused occasionally and then doubled in force.

An uncomfortable numbness seeped in from her fingers and toes by the time she dressed. Fear.

Now she heard a muffled voice yelling. Her heart jumped.

She'd know that voice anywhere. What was Tanner doing here?

She shuffled out into the main room. Orange-yellow light flowed in through the front windows in large squares, obliterating any color that the little tree had had. The next knock made her jump. It was Tanner, but it wasn't her house. She wouldn't get the door. Something in his tone froze her blood.

From around the corner came Seth, sleepy, rubbing his eye, dressed in a gray T-shirt he'd obviously slept in. He stretched his eyes and mouth open, getting ready to see what the commotion was about. Seeing her near the hallway opening, he splayed one hand in her direction. *No closer.*

Between a bout of knocks, Seth opened the door, squaring himself in front of the opening. "Good morning," he said pointedly.

"Where is she?" Tanner roared, ignoring Seth's barrier and coming in. He was so physical and large, coming into spaces he shouldn't, that he seemed dangerous enough to fill the room. His arms could come into her space or Seth's at any moment. Something about his clumsy violence told her he had to be drunk. Mixed with her fear was sadness. She'd seen the good side of him. But she didn't know this monster at all.

"Where—there she is!" He pointed at her.

Her breath seized.

"Lex, come with me!"

She didn't know what to do besides press her back into the wall. Stacey growled low beside her.

Seth stepped quickly between them. "Miss Schmitt can do what she likes."

"You mean you?" Tanner snarled, and then cursed. He looked at Lexi over Seth's shoulder. "Jesse told me he saw you. Is *this* why you broke up with me?"

Lexi realized she had bare feet. For some reason, the fact deeply embarrassed her. "No!" she said. "You cheated on me. What else was I supposed to do?"

"Then what is this?" He came forward like a bull, disregarding anything in his way.

Seth stopped his advance, two hands on Tanner's shoulder. Tanner tried to shrug him off and keep going. Seth didn't let go. Enraged, Tanner swatted at Seth's hands. When Seth fought to keep holding him back, Tanner pushed him with close-quarters violence that made Lexi catch her breath. Seth and Tanner scuffled. No big moves, just hatred and ferocity. The sweaty fight was worse than if one had punched the other in the face. They knocked around the room, scooting the couch, tipping over the tree.

Finally, Seth, the smaller of the two, shoved Tanner away from him. "Get out of my house," he said.

Tanner hurled a curse at him. "Then get off my case."

Seth stilled oddly at that. The poised intensity he'd carried the last few minutes snapped like broken elastic. The head hole on his T-shirt, stretched out from the fight, gaped to the side.

Tanner tried one more time. "Lex?" When she didn't respond, he set his jaw in a cruel, belligerent way. She watched his hands for fists. He didn't swing them. She thought he might spit. "She's a cheater. If you want her, you can have her."

He crashed open the screen door on his way out.

Lexi felt air return to the room. Blood filled her cheeks.

At the door, Seth watched Tanner go. He stood there for a while with the door open. The air that flowed into the house was icy cold. Part of her wanted to say something about how cold she was, but she couldn't interrupt his thoughts. What was he thinking? Seth was all energy, but now he was quiet. Too quiet. She waited to move until he did.

The silence took on different dimensions the longer they both stood there, unmoving. One awkwardness would resolve, and then another loud one would rush in like a cold wave. She shivered.

Seth closed the door. The room didn't feel any warmer. Slowly, he righted Ginger Ann and walked past her back to his room.

Miserable, she stayed for a little longer. The wood floor was uneven and rough under her bare feet. The little gingerbread house looked even littler in the daylight. They had just put the roof on and left it undecorated last night. Like the tree. Its prickly, twiggy arms mocked her. She couldn't eat pancakes now even if they were put in front of her. Her stomach felt too hollow and sick. This sickness was a different kind than when she had seen Tanner with another girl. This felt more like shame than sadness.

If you want her, you can have her.

Maybe he was right. Maybe she was a cheater. She had felt something with Seth so soon after she broke up with Tanner, after all. But she hadn't planned to forge a connection with someone so quickly. He was funny, and generous, and hardworking, and kind. His wide, sudden smile made her smile too. She wanted to cause more of those smiles.

Forcing herself to move, she went around the couch to Ginger Ann, touching first the fabric couch cover and then the sharp pine needles. The touch grounded her.

A step echoed behind her. She turned to see Neal, dressed for the day in a fine vest, probably what Santa wore when it wasn't Christmas Eve.

"Oh, good morning!" He beamed at her.

Tears started in her eyes. "Did you hear all that?" she asked.

He tipped his mouth kindly. "Some of it. You'd better go talk to him."

She dropped her eyes. He was right. "Okay," she muttered, trudging past the kitchen.

"First on the left," Neal called after her.

Good thing he did. She had no idea which room was Seth's. Thankfully, the door was ajar. Seth sat on the edge of his bed, staring at his phone. It seemed as though he had been weighing his options since the fight ended, though she wasn't sure what those options were. He ran his thumb along the side of the phone, brows furrowed.

She knocked on the open door before entering.

He waved her in. "It's not your fault," he said quickly without looking at her, as though that would solve everything.

"I'm still sorry." She came in and sat beside him. Her hands lay folded in her lap. "Thanks for… standing up for me."

He hummed, still looking at the phone.

She didn't know what she'd expected, but it must have involved looking at her, because she was disappointed and annoyed that he didn't. "I had no idea he was coming," she said.

"He's my biggest client," he said. The pent-up words came out in a rush. "We're *this* close to winning a suit. There's nothing in the agreement that requires him to stay with me." He chewed the inside of his cheek.

She didn't know what to say. "Can you save it?"

His eyelashes fluttered distractedly. "I don't know. I don't know if I can."

Shame crept over her again, now burning and sticky like tar.

"I should try to do *something*." With the word, he waved his phone in the air.

"Yeah, call them up," she said, but her voice sounded small and empty.

He let out a breath. "I don't know if I should call Mr. Bingham quite yet. It's Christmas morning. Maybe he doesn't know what Tanner was doing."

It was Christmas morning. She had forgotten.

"Yeah." Was she hoping that Seth would keep defending her, comfort her maybe?

Seth scrubbed his knuckles over his hair. "I should give him a call." He opened the phone screen and started dialing. Before Mr. Bingham answered, he hung up and looked at Lexi.

She took the hint. "I can go, if you need to—"

"No no no. I don't know that I want to do business with them. It's just…" He squeezed his eyes shut. "It's just so much money."

"I think," she replied, "I'm going to go help your dad with breakfast." She still didn't feel like eating breakfast, but she had to get out of there and let Seth make his own decisions. She had royally screwed things up for him.

His biggest client. She sucked in a long, shaky breath.

Definitely not a Hallmark movie.

Santa had a cup of coffee waiting for her when she emerged back into the kitchen.

She was struck anew by the couch, now slightly askew, and Ginger Ann, now with fewer needles on one side. The room remembered the scuffle.

She could barely taste the coffee. Neal evidently knew better than to try to talk to her. They drank from their mugs in silence.

One more day.

One more day and she could get out of Tall Pine and leave all these horrible memories behind her.

Mostly horrible memories.

Coffee swirled around the bottom of her cup, circling like her thoughts. Tanner, the breakup, Seth, the fight, the almost-kiss…

Seth came out of his room, looking drawn. Lexi gripped her mug tighter.

Neal didn't have to ask his son if he wanted coffee. The mug was automatic. Seth took it with a grateful look as he sat opposite her.

She hid behind her cup, gazing studiously into the last sip pooling at the bottom. More and more, she felt the weight of being unwanted. Here it was, Christmas morning, and she sat with two strangers who had agreed to take her in, and jumpstart her car, and feed her meals, and buy manky Christmas trees to keep her happy, and now her ex-boyfriend had disrupted their holiday by picking a fight. She curled her feet toward each other under the chair.

Seth smiled at his dad. It still looked artless, but his eyes were distracted and upset. "Merry Christmas, Dad."

Out of habit or the holiday, Neal laughed like Santa.

Seth sprang out of his chair, spreading his nervous energy over the kitchen. He shuffled through dishes and ingredients until he had eggs and toast cooking for them all. Neal didn't offer to help. The wise look in his eye warned Lexi to leave him alone too. Seth needed to work by himself just now.

The smell of hot butter filled the space. Maybe she was a little hungry after all.

A few minutes later, Seth set plates down in front of them, the clatter loud in the quiet.

"Jam?" he asked.

"Yes, please," Neal replied, unflustered and expansive.

Seth brought that too. He ate rapidly, standing up.

Lexi had hardly taken more than two bites of her crunchy toast when he announced, "I'm going to take a shower." And he left.

Neal sighed. "He'll be all right," he said.

"I don't know," she replied once she was sure Seth was safely behind a closed door. "How big is the Bingham account?"

Neal knit his eyebrows. "How do you know about that?"

"He told me. Maybe he shouldn't have, but he told me."

"He's worked only on the Bingham case for the past few months. It's a small town and their business is enormous. They need him. They wouldn't fire him."

"So you heard?"

"I heard." He seemed awfully calm. Maybe he hadn't caught

the tone of Tanner's voice. She knew Tanner best. He was done with Seth and done with her.

"I, um… I'm going to take a walk. It looks nice outside," she said. It didn't. It looked cold. The sky was blue, though, so maybe Neal bought her excuse.

"It does," Neal agreed. The way he said it reminded her of when they first met. He knew more than he said, but he didn't say it.

She got ready quickly, leaving most of her breakfast uneaten. With her out of their hair, they could exchange presents or whatever they normally did on Christmas. And she could set things right. Neal gave her a warm smile, dimples rising above the beard, as she left the house.

It didn't take her long to find the Binghams' address in her phone.

0.79 miles. A short walk. A cold one, though. The morning was silent in a way few mornings were. Everyone stayed in their houses. The forest around her seemed to absorb every noise but the occasional dropping pine cone.

She couldn't just call Tanner. That would do more harm than good. She had to talk to Mr. Bingham. He was the owner of the company, so he probably made these kinds of decisions. Without his number, she had no choice but to show up at his door.

Seth didn't deserve to lose his job because of her. He was angry, and rightfully so. He had chosen his job over her, and rightfully so. She would make sure the damage wasn't irreparable.

Her stomach clenched the closer she got to the house. The house where she had thought she'd be welcome, where she had planned to stay with her future in-laws.

Be brave. Be brave.

Among the trees rose a large log house. It looked exactly like the pictures. It was far more expensive-looking than the house on Pinewood Way. The walls rose taller has she approached. No, she just felt smaller. She tucked her short hair behind her ear, untucked it again.

Maybe this wasn't a good idea. Why would they listen to her? If she defended Seth too vigorously, maybe they'd all think she cheated on Tanner. Besides, she was Tanner's ex—she had no voice with these people.

But she had to try. Seth deserved it.

Mouth dusty dry, she knocked on the large front door, avoiding the full evergreen wreath that hung from it.

In no time at all, Mrs. Bingham answered. She wore a smile, but it was a plastic mask. "Hello, Alexis," she said. "What… are you doing here?"

Lexi tried to swallow. She began carefully. "I saw Tanner this morning. He, um, he indicated that he wanted to, uh, fire your lawyer. Just because he was… being nice to me. I wanted to talk to Mr. Bingham for a minute to make sure he doesn't lose his job, if that's okay."

Mrs. Bingham's mouth was a small bead of annoyance. "It's Christmas morning, and we can make our own decisions."

"But—"

"It's not your business, Alexis," she said firmly. "This is a personal matter and you made it very clear that you don't want to be involved in this family anymore."

"Lexi?" This was a new voice.

Seth.

He took huge, powerful steps toward her. He must have walked the whole way with that kind of intensity. "Mrs. Bingham," he greeted.

Mrs. Bingham opened the door a fraction wider. "Seth, I don't think you should be—"

"Excuse me. I just wanted to come and personally resign from your case. The way Tanner has treated me, has treated Lexi, demonstrates a lack of integrity that I can't bring myself to defend."

"That was one person," Lexi said quietly. "The whole family needs your help."

"He indicated that he would like to terminate this working relationship as well," he replied, half to her and half to Mrs. Bingham.

"You don't have to," Lexi insisted.

"Yes, I do."

Mr. Bingham appeared at the door. Lexi's heart stalled.

"I quit," Seth said.

"Seth!" Lexi cried.

"Sir, I can't work for you anymore. I wish you the best on your case."

"What is this?" Mr. Bingham demanded.

Mrs. Bingham turned to her husband. "Tanner went over there," she said in a confidential way, as though even that didn't concern the two people on the front porch.

"Yes, he did. And so I'm quitting."

"Enough of this," Mr. Bingham said. "Seth, I'll call you tomorrow." His gaze was pointed.

They shut the door.

Lexi whirled on Seth. "What are you doing?" she hissed. "They're your biggest client!"

He half-shrugged, more of a twitch of his shoulders. "He treated you like dirt."

"But I'm leaving and you'll still be here." *I'm nobody. I'm a secondary character.*

He grew still as he had after Tanner stormed out.

Finally, he said, "I don't care."

"About which part?"

"I don't care," he repeated, all eloquence gone. The stubborn repetition meant he really had made up his mind. He was quitting no matter what she said.

"Are you—?"

"I'm sure."

She searched his face. "You weren't sure earlier."

"Of course not! This isn't a Hallmark movie. I couldn't make a decision immediately." He let out a helpless laugh. "It's a lot of money."

She felt the same laugh tug at her lips.

He sighed and then squinted with mock seriousness. Light danced in his eyes. "Can I kiss you now?"

She only got in one of her rapid nods.

It had been a while since someone kissed her like that, tenderly, passionately. He knew her and wanted to know her more.

He backed away and beamed one of his wide, sudden, joyful grins. She grinned back. This felt right.

"I think," she said with a small shiver, "I think Santa's waiting for us back at the house."

"And Arnold." He turned and offered his arm.

She took it. "Ginger Ann," she corrected.

"I'll have to thank him," he said, meaning his dad.

"For what?" she asked. She squeezed his arm as they walked carefully down the porch steps. The stairs weren't too icy, but neither of them was in a hurry.

"For inviting you over when you were stranded."

Her cheeks warmed. "I'm still stranded."

"I'll see if I can pop your tire or something. Keep you here a little longer." He winked at her. His wavy hair looked golden in the morning sun. "Or a lot longer."

She pursed her lips in a smile. His biggest client was gone. She was just a receptionist back home, easily replaceable. They walked as though they both knew how spontaneous and uprooted they were. "I'd like that."

He bent to kiss her again. "Merry Christmas, Lexi," he said.

"Merry Christmas, Seth."

SASHA AND THE CHRISTMAS LIST

THE LIST AND THE RULE

Sasha Combs bent over the blue-lit screen. Her niece's new drawing blurred as she held it too close to the camera. Even though Sasha leaned closer, the screen was just a riot of green and red.

"You have to hold it like this," she heard her sister Marie say. Graceful bronze hands came into the frame and adjusted the picture. Santa Claus came into focus. "Ask your aunty Sasha if she can tell what it is," Marie whispered.

"What is it?" Emma, her niece, held up the piece proudly. Wild flyaway hairs had come loose from her dark braids. They glowed in the early morning light streaming through the windows behind her.

Before Sasha could answer, a shorthaired pointer ambled into the scene amid a scream of giggles. Warner, Marie's younger daughter, tumbled out of the way of the dog, knocking into her sister who still gripped the drawing in one hand.

Sasha adjusted her crossed legs as she waited for the commotion to settle down on the other end of the video call. The peppermint stick one of her students had given her before going on Christmas Break clicked as she moved it to her other cheek.

She'd sucked it to a deadly point but couldn't resist testing its sharpness against her tongue.

"Still there, Sasha?" Marie asked, tilting the camera so her face came into the frame.

"Still here."

"How late is it there?"

"It's, uh…"

Marie's eyes rolled up as she did the math. A gasp showed she'd reached the conclusion. "It's nearly two o' clock there! You should have said something. We need to figure out a better time to do these calls." Her two girls and the dog ran by in the background, distracted by something more fun. Marie beamed. "At least you're on Christmas Break, right?"

Sasha flexed her foot against the comforter. "Yeah, but I still have to go in tomorrow to tear down the set."

"It's Saturday!"

"I'm a teacher. There wasn't any time after the performance tonight." There actually had been, but all the students and parents were too anxious to start their vacation.

"Will you have any help, at least?"

Sasha, at all of five foot one, could hardly carry off the set pieces herself, regardless of the planks and crunches she did a couple times a week. Her dark arms were getting toned, though, she noticed with satisfaction. "Yeah, there's one other guy," she said. "Jonas Harper. You met him. He helped build the set, so he has a better idea of how to dismantle it."

"Ooh, yes." Marie waggled her eyebrows. "He's that other teacher?"

Sasha ignored the hint. "Fifth grade, but he comes up to the junior high building for stuff like this."

"Does he have a girlfriend?"

"Stop!" Jonas, with cheekbones sharp enough to make award-winning black and white photos, was fairly gorgeous – all the junior high girls tittered when he was around – but he was also one of Sasha's best friends. It didn't matter that unwanted feelings sometimes reared their ugly heads when she was around him. She couldn't jeopardize one of her only close friendships by becoming more than friends.

Sasha's romances never turned out anyway. They always ended in messy tears and *Singin' in the Rain*. It was a cliché, and that made her feel worse. She didn't know how to keep a man interested. She was cute, not hot; she worked long hours; she forgot anniversaries. So her career became her focus. No romantic relationships. Especially not with Jonas Harper.

"I don't know. I think you two would be cute together. And… honestly, if we're not there, I want to think that you have some people around you, you know, for the holidays."

"I have people."

"Besides Margot." Sasha's bespectacled roommate.

Sasha sighed and pierced her tongue on the peppermint.

The camera angle listed to the side as Marie stood. "So, the performance went well?"

A smile dashed across Sasha's face at the memory. The sweaty, hairspray high of the final theatre presentation still hadn't washed off. "Wonderfully! Alex even resisted the urge to follow through on his closing night plan."

"Mm?"

"Don't ask."

Remembering the performance almost chased away the lump in her throat that had lodged there ever since she started this call with her sister. Sasha couldn't pretend that they were still in the US now, not since Christmas Break had started. Now she had to face the fact that she'd be doing Christmas alone. Even Sasha's roommate was leaving for a week. The prospect made her belt out "Defying Gravity" in the car and eat too many peppermint sticks. Now that it was so late, she had reached the fragile state when any heartfelt commercial could make her cry.

"I'm so glad it went well," Marie crooned. "Ah, we miss you!"

Sasha couldn't respond. She just sucked her peppermint stick in a desperate attempt to pretend that her sister hadn't been transferred to the base in Germany just in time for the holidays.

"Warner is practicing for the Christmas pageant at our new church here. Since we came after they started practicing, she gets to be a sheep."

"Baaa," from the background.

"Exactly, sweetie." Marie looked back into the camera at Sasha. "The List won't be the same without you."

The List was the complicated set of holiday traditions that the sisters had built over the years. There were so many that they rarely did every one. The past few years, the List had tipped in favor of Emma and Warner. To Sasha, the List *was* Christmas. Now, with her family thousands of miles away, she wouldn't have much of a Christmas at all.

"Yeah," Sasha murmured.

Marie's lips settled into a bossy line that Sasha knew well. "Okay, it's too late for you to be staying up. Go to bed! I have to get the kids ready for Christmas shopping anyway. The Christmas markets here are beautiful, Sash. You'd love them. I'm hanging up now."

"Okay. Tell the kids I love them."

Goodbyes were followed by a blank screen. Sasha bit off the sharp tip of her peppermint stick and laid her fist against her mouth, staring emptily at the place where her sister had been.

She would not cry. If she did, her roommate would hear and knock on the door to see what was wrong.

The time on her phone glowed 1:57. Marie was probably right. With her rigid military discipline, she usually was. There was truth in art and beauty too, Sasha tried to remind her. But in the midst of an argument, art and beauty usually lost to cold common sense. Right now, that common sense was telling her to brush her teeth and get some sleep. It would be another early morning.

TEARING DOWN THE SET

Bleary-eyed, clutching a Star Wars travel mug full of hot coffee, Sasha arrived at the school theatre the next morning. Marie had been right. 2:00 AM was too late. She winced at the clanking that sounded from the stage through the empty auditorium. Tinny Christmas music played from Jonas' iPhone.

Sasha climbed the steps to find him hunched behind the town's brightly painted "workshop," which had been wheeled to the wings with the other big pieces. "Morning," she said. "How do you always get here before me? You live farther away."

"Morning." He didn't look up, instead straining with a bolt near the wheels. It was strange to see him in jeans and tennis shoes. Even when they hung out after work, they both wore their professional teacher attire. His white and blue flannel shirt, collar askew beneath his brown hair, was rolled up to the elbows, exposing a sunburst tattoo dark against the light skin near the crook of his elbow. "Did you use super glue on this?" he grunted. "Steady it for me, would you?"

Sasha set her cup down beside an open cellophane package of treats she'd given to all the students the night before. Briony must have left hers. She was always leaving things in the classroom. Sasha removed her gloves to hold up the plywood. After a few seconds, the bolt came loose.

"There!" Jonas cried, standing to ease the building façade to the floor.

"How long have you been here?" She scooped up the coffee again, holding it protectively against her face before taking a sip.

"Just half an hour or so. Not long."

Together, they repeated the process of dismantling the set without discussing more than where to hold, what to undo, and where to lay the boards. They'd worked together enough times that they already knew what to do. Jonas was the carpenter and the muscle. Sasha was the manual assistant and director. Easy.

"Oh, I always thought this version was weird," Sasha exclaimed, as "Silent Night" by The Temptations warbled through Jonas' phone. Her family had owned the album when she was a kid, but she and her sister used to make fun of the song, singing along with all their might, adding runs like Mariah. She burst into a solo rendition, hitting all the high notes behind the narration at the beginning.

Jonas straightened, with an amused grin. His usually cleanly shaved face looked shadowy with stubble.

Marie's part came, and Sasha stopped.

"That's good," he exclaimed. "I always forget you can sing."

She nudged him. "Oh, thanks! It's not like I head the musical theatre department or anything."

"Maybe you were just telling the kids how to sing. I don't know," he teased. "I'm over in the fifth-grade world. My limit is Jingle Bells, and even that's sketchy."

Sasha tipped her travel mug back and forth. No more coffee. "My sister and I used to sing that song all the time."

"Is that the sister I met?"

"Yeah. Marie. Now it's… something we do every year." *Not anymore.* The thought made her melancholy. Tearing down the set was the last buffer between her and Christmas Break spent without her sister. "She just moved to Germany."

Jonas raised an eyebrow. "Military?"

Sasha nodded. Moves like that were common enough in Colorado. "We used to spend Christmas together, so..." She tossed her head like a horse ridding itself of a fly. "It's fine. That was one of the things on the List we made."

He rolled his eyes. "Of course. You have to have a list."

"Yes, of course!" Sasha was the organized artsy type, if that was a type. She always came to rehearsals with a list scrawled on a scrap of paper, and she stuck to the numbered items as if they were law.

"A list of Christmas things? Like traditions?" He positioned himself on one side of the plank depicting a cabin in the woods. Sasha took the other side. "Ready? One, two, three..."

They lifted and started to trundle awkwardly down the ramp to the theatre closet, holding the set piece between them.

"Yeah," Sasha huffed. "Like traditions."

"And singing that version of Silent Night made the list? This has to be specific."

They didn't talk for a few more seconds because they had to wrestle the wooden façade upright to get it through the oversized door. No hint of the Christmas music reached them in the supply closet, as though the stuffy smell in there also insulated against noises from the outside world. Sasha was hired three years ago and still hadn't explored all the recesses. Props and sets and costumes from old productions of *Hello, Dolly!* and *Fiddler on the Roof* peeked out from behind brown cardboard boxes. One day she'd get to it all. Maybe the next couple weeks would be a good time with the kids gone on break.

"Do they leave the doors unlocked for the next couple weeks?" she asked. The maintenance and security teams normally had hours during the summer when teachers could enter the school, but she'd never thought about it in December. Too much on the List to bother with extra schoolwork.

Jonas gave her a disbelieving look, sweeping his hands against each other as they headed back to gather more. He still hadn't fixed the collar of his shirt. It angled up on one side. "No," he said. "Don't even think about coming in after today. You already work too hard."

"So do–"

"And you can't deflect that easily." He veered in front of her and walked backward up the ramp leading back to the stage to he could face her. "Tell me about this list."

Sasha exhaled slowly. Jonas was tenacious and patient. He'd wheedle the details from her eventually. "Don't you have Christmas traditions?"

"Oh, yeah. My brother and I play basketball on Christmas Eve after we open presents."

"Outside?" In December? In Colorado? The very idea appalled. She pulled a candy cane out of her pocket and peeled off the wrapping. Never too early for peppermint.

He laughed. "Yeah. I think it started when I was eight and got a basketball for Christmas. Will and I put on our snowsuits and played HORSE."

Now that he explained it, that didn't surprise her as much. Jonas was always up for adventure. He liked novelty, and it took something truly awful before he'd complain. Once, they'd gone to happy hour together after a particularly grueling week of work. He wanted a whiskey neat. Something about the way he ordered it made Sasha's stomach swoop unexpectedly, even before the drinks came. That was the first time she feared she had accidentally caught feelings for her friend. So she'd spent the rest of the time seeking out his flaws – he'd done a terrible job shaving that morning if the hairs by his lip were any indication, he'd never heard of the musical *Wicked*, his armpits were sweaty after the long day, he flirted back with the waitress... But the worst thing was that the very same waitress who leaned suggestively toward him, eyes glittering, didn't get him the whiskey neat he ordered, but some beer on tap. He shrugged it off. Then the bill came, and it included the order of the people sitting next to them, who had gotten fried pickles and cheesy bread. Sasha, unreasonably angry by this time, hailed the waitress. When she arrived, all smiles and cleavage, Jonas didn't complain about any of the mistakes. He was too forbearing, in her opinion. Forgiving yet tenacious. A contradiction, like Sasha.

"Well, that sounds freezing," she said.

"It's fun."

"Who wins?"

"Will did, until I got older." He flashed a smile. It was artless and smudgy with work. Those cheekbones made the smile a work of art.

Sasha's heart gave a little twist. She frowned and angrily chewed off the end of the candy cane. *No no no!*

"But you're still avoiding the question," he finished. "What about this list?"

The music had moved on from the Temptations to Ariana Grande. All this music used to swell her soul with the twinkling warmth of Christmas, but now the songs felt hollowed out. Just notes she could play on a xylophone. The magic at the center had dried up.

She hooked her finger around the candy cane and removed it from her mouth. Jonas shifted his weight, apparently sensing her seriousness. "There are fifty-six items."

He burst out in a guffaw. "Fifty-six?"

She glowered at him, more irritated than she should be. He was helping her, after all. "Yes. Do you want me to tell you, or…?"

"Go ahead. Do you have them all memorized?" He set his mouth in a mock serious line.

Don't look at his lips. "Not in order! No need to be that way. It's written down somewhere." She knew exactly where – her childhood journal, but she wasn't about to admit that. Versions of *Dear Diary, what a day! Today I got the role in the school play and kissed Tony Prentiss* would play through his mind, no doubt. At least they would play through hers if he had admitted to keeping a childhood diary. The worst part was that those guesses wouldn't be too far off in her case. Cliché again. She sighed.

One of Jonas' eyebrows arched. His warm brown eyes searched hers. Sasha never was very good at hiding her emotions, and Jonas was perceptive enough to see that something was going on. To his credit, he didn't ask. "What are some of the other things you always do? You know, besides singing along to the Temptations?"

"We have to watch *The Muppet Christmas Carol* and *Whose Line is It Anyway.*"

"The show with the improv?"

"And an episode of *Psych.*"

His eyes went wide in a helpless question.

"The detective show," she clarified. "He's a pretend psychic and they solve crimes… No?"

He shook his head, obvious amusement on his face. "So, you watch all these things – some of which are not Christmasy, by the way – and then what?"

"We make a huge paper lantern. It's usually too big to fly." She chuckled, despite herself. "And if it caught fire, that wouldn't be good, so ours just stays on the ground. It's a Filipino thing. My mom's Filipino," she explained. Most people assumed both her parents were black.

"Okay."

"I'm not sure how far you want me to go," she continued. "My nieces love it when we drink cider and watch the snow, so that's on the List. The most important thing is on Christmas Eve. We bring homemade ornaments to a craft fair. It's a whole thing. Snazzy fundraiser. We know the people who go every year. We don't have our own booth or anything, but we give our ornaments to my grandmother and then go shopping and dancing." She faded off, cleared her throat, and indicated the next set piece at her feet. "We should take another one."

They lifted it and headed back to the closet. "But your sister's in Germany now," Jonas said in a quiet voice.

"Mm hm." Sasha couldn't manage more. She hadn't even decorated her apartment yet. Margot had put up a few things, but it looked nothing like the usual Christmas explosion Sasha let loose around the holidays.

It was close to midday by the time they finished putting away the rest of the set and sweeping the stage. Christmas Break loomed in front of her, with nothing to block her thoughts from the lonely weeks ahead. She put on her gloves with a furious tug.

"Hey, Sasha."

She turned to see Jonas landing gracefully after jumping off the stage.

"Do you want to get some cider? Like, not…" He rubbed the back of his neck with one hand and picked up his jacket from a seat back with the other. "But just to check off one of the things from your list. It's too bad your sister can't be here."

The rush of warmth to her cheeks was alarming. *He all but said this wasn't a date. Get ahold of yourself.* "Is it snowing?" she hedged, taking off one glove to check her phone. The weather app affirmed it was.

She bit her lip. It was risky. Every guy she'd fallen for – *every one* – had found her not good enough when they got to know her. Friendship was safe. A relationship was not. So, she wouldn't hope for this to turn into a relationship, even though Jonas was sweet and handsome and good with kids and listened when she–

She shook her head. "Yes. Yes, let's do it. Thank you."

His smile tugged slowly at his face as though he guessed what she was thinking.

"So let's get going," she said, grabbing her Star Wars mug and sweeping past him to hide her blush.

CIDER

Sasha hadn't realized how difficult it was to find cider. It was Christmastime. Every restaurant would sell cider, right? No. Either they were out of stock, or else they offered hot chocolate instead – another great option, if the goal weren't checking something off her official Christmas List.

Target still had powdered cider in stock. Jonas, as usual, didn't complain about the substitute. Instead, he grabbed the box from the shelf and waggled it in her face. "Will this do?"

No sat on the tip of her tongue, but she took a deep breath and nodded. It was kind of Jonas to help, so she could stow away her dramatic tendencies.

"Good," he said, striding through the aisle toward the cash registers. "At least we finally found some!"

Afternoon sun blared through the automatic doors. Sasha regarded it mournfully. "Yes," she agreed. "Warner and Emma do this at night so they can see the snow under the streetlamps. Marie lets them stay up late that night."

They found a station at the self-checkout. A five-dollar bill appeared like a coin in a magician's hand.

"Wait!" Sasha objected. "This is my List. I should probably get that."

"It costs two dollars." He shrugged. The bill was already getting sucked into the machine. "And I suggested that we do this, so…" After a clink of change in the automatic cup, he scooped up the box of powdered cider and nodded to the attendant at the door as they passed on the way out.

"Why do you always do that?"

The plastic lining of his coat made a zipping sound as he turned. "Do what?"

She squinted against the sunlight. Jonas moved to block the glare. It was such an automatic gesture that she was momentarily speechless. Also, it was cold and Jonas was standing very close, so those things could have contributed. Gathering herself, she answered, "I was going to say, 'Drop off your sentences.' I'm always telling the students not to do that. But I mean getting the cider, offering to come with me…"

"You dropped off your sentence." His brown eyes laughed.

She huffed. "That was… that was for dramatic effect!"

"I know how you love that." His lips twitched, but he didn't laugh at her.

"Hm, yes." How was she supposed to take that? She knew she could be dramatic, and organized, and passionate, and a whole bunch of other things. He teased her about it at practices, but here it felt more like flirting than when middle-schoolers were there. *There's no harm in it, Sasha. He's just your friend. Doing a favor. Just like Margot would.* Maybe she'd see if Margot wanted to do some of the other items on the List. Of course, the way things were going, all the items would turn out disastrously. The number of stores *without* apple cider still staggered her.

Jonas shifted his weight. "You just seemed really disappointed not to be able to do these things with your sister, and I had time, and nobody should feel lonely at the holidays, if, you know, you can do something about it." He shrugged again, the casual, one-shouldered shrug that was his trademark.

Emotions pushed against her throat. "I'm not lonely," she said, taking the box from him and walking to the car.

Good one. 'I'm not looking for a boyfriend, thanks. What you're doing is essentially meaningless.' Why did she always say the first thing that came to mind when she wanted to get out of an awkward situation? Too often, it just made the situation worse.

Jonas caught up easily. Those long legs. Opening the car door and ducking into the driver's seat beside her, he said, "That's not what I…"

She bit her lip to stop herself from pointing out that he'd faded out again.

For a split second, his eyes dipped to her lips. Heat flamed along her neck, chasing away the cold. She stopped biting them, instead pursing them together in a way she hoped was unappealing. He turned the ignition.

"I just thought this would be fun," Jonas amended. "But we do need some hot water."

"Yes," she said, grasping at the new task with unwarranted excitement. He side-eyed her. She widened her eyes in challenge.

"Do you think a sink will be hot enough?"

"Probably not." She remembered having cider like this out of scalding metal tureens the church put out after Christmas service. If those were the standard, then they needed water heated by Vulcan's forge.

"I have a hotpot at home." Pausing at a stop sign, he pointed down the street.

In their quest to find cider, they'd gone farther and farther from town. Jonas lived in the mountainous foothills of Woodland Park, and they actually had traveled almost all the way there.

Sasha pressed her fingertip against the pointy edge of the box of cider powder. She had been to his house before, but always for work parties, or gatherings with a few friends. Never alone.

She was overthinking. Her specialty. Despite her better judgment, she studied his face for a sign of his intentions. The cut jaw and lopsided collar gave away nothing.

Taking on the air of someone much less neurotic, someone who saw the invitation as just an invitation and not an *invitation*, she leaned back in the seat. Her hand found the seatbelt, pulling it in and out as though to test for good craftsmanship. "Yeah, sure, of course. It's close? Sure, that's a good idea. Yeah, let's go there. We'll get the water, yes, for sure."

Perfectly normal.

"If you don't want to go…" he said, turning onto the road. He didn't seem offended or freaked out by her bizarre behavior.

Even after all the time they'd spent together, she'd never noticed how often he left his sentences unfinished.

"No, I do. I think it's a good plan. If we don't get the water, then we can't check the item off the list, right?"

He smiled. "Right."

Jonas lived in a little home tucked into trees, more suburban than most homes in Woodland Park. Patches of white snow lay on his front lawn and on top of the mailbox that read "Harper" down the side. By the front door lounged a couple gnome statues of that had clearly been moldering there for years, maybe even before Jonas moved in.

He had a roommate named Craig, a mountainy sort of person with a long beard that made him look ten years older, but there was no other car in the driveway.

Moments later, they stood on that little front porch with steaming mugs of cider in their hands. It was surprisingly palatable. The smell, at least, was appetizing. Of course, that would have been true of just about anything, since the protein bar she'd eaten in the car that morning hadn't filled her up. Standing there, looking out at the residential street, her internal outburst of emotions made less sense. Now, she felt peaceful. There was no need to panic about Jonas. They were friends, good friends, even when her hormones pointed out his muscled forearms or bari-tone voice. All she had to do was not let things get weird between them. If she succeeded, they could have a good Christmas after all, or at least one not quite so hopeless as she'd feared.

"Okay, it isn't nighttime." His voice cut into her thoughts. "The cider is a little weird. I'm not your niece. Anything else I should know about how I'm doing this wrong?" he teased, taking a sip. His eye twitched when the burning liquid hit his mouth. The freezing breeze would cool the drink down in no time.

"You didn't do it wrong." She smiled apologetically. "Thanks for getting the cider. This is really nice."

"Yeah, not the worst. Oh!" He lowered his mug. "Did Alex do that thing on closing night? I didn't see it." Jonas usually came to the opening performances, not closing ones.

"No," she sighed in relief.

Jonas rolled his eyes in mock consternation. "That kid…"

"Right?"

"I was a lot like him when I was his age, but I would have done it."

"What?" Sasha couldn't picture it. Alex was so tightly wound, trying to impress his classmates with random shenanigans. Jonas, on the other hand, acted so laid back.

He raised an eyebrow. "I was. I thought I was hilarious."

"You are hilarious." She held up a gloved hand to correct herself. "Sometimes. Sometimes you're hilarious."

"Did you hear the knock-knock joke about the KGB?"

"Stop!" She pushed him and he laughed, wavering good-naturedly on his feet.

"I was a bad kid."

"Alex isn't a bad kid. He's just… spirited."

"Then I was a spirited kid."

Sasha hazarded a sip from the mug. Just right. Now, if it were only snowing with her family here, everything would be perfect.

"I like how you deal with the spirited kids," Jonas continued, still saying the word *spirited* as though it wasn't his own. "My teachers didn't know what to do with me, but you can correct them without having them feel…" He shrugged a shoulder.

The compliment warmed her insides. Jonas had seen her direct kids dozens of times as he built sets for their performances. "Aw, thanks," she said. "I'm sure you weren't that bad." It suddenly hit her that she'd never seen him teach his class of fifth graders. The image pleased her. Mr. Harper. She had no doubt that he was entertaining and kind.

"You underestimate me, Combs."

She rounded on him. "Give me an example, then."

He pushed out his lips in an exaggerated thinking face. "Okay, okay. We had a substitute."

"Oh no…"

"Oh yes. We had a substitute. I was in middle school, and I thought it would be awesome if we all called each other by different names. Innocuous enough, right?"

"Right," she answered tentatively.

"The girl in front of me, Mindy Grant, wouldn't play. During roll call, she kept yelling that her name was Mindy, even when the rest of us shouted her down and called her Bindy. The whole thing got out of hand. Mindy and the sub were both crying by the end."

"Bindy? What about Cindy?"

"I was in middle school!" he cried. "I wasn't feeling very creative, apparently."

"They were crying over that?" Sasha had diffused a hundred situations more volatile than that.

"There was a can of soda involved."

"Ah. Mindy?"

He dropped his head. "Mindy."

"I'm surprised you sacrificed it. I guarded my Dr. Pepper in seventh grade like cans were fifty bucks a pop."

He chuckled and took another swig of cider. "I didn't exactly think it through. Things just happened, and I'd realize it later."

She shook her head. "I don't understand that at all."

Sasha couldn't have been more different in junior high. Her habit of overanalyzing and dramatizing had morphed into more helpful avenues as she grew up, but it was still a struggle.

He narrowed his eyes. "You've never done anything on impulse before? I find that hard to believe."

"Never." She stood to her full height in front of him, the image (she felt) of propriety, like a librarian. She came up to Jonas' nose.

"All the Christmas traditions," he said, nodding thoughtfully.

"Lists all the time." She waved her hand and turned back to the snow-spotted lawn. "You've seen them." And there were some that nobody had seen: saddest songs, pretty words in Armenian, best episodes of *Gilmore Girls* ranked, a bucket list if she found out she only had eight weeks to live, most attractive characteristics in men...

"Well, I think," he said, "especially with your family moving away, you have to embrace some of the change."

His tone was teacherly. Maybe this was his Mr. Harper voice. She only hummed.

"Really, I think you should do something impulsive."

She held up her mug. "This doesn't count?"

"Doing something you've done every year at the same time?"

"In a different way!"

He gave her an indulgent look and pointedly finished his cider. His face contorted. "It gets worse at the end."

She grimaced and held out her cup. "I'm starting to notice." Chalky powder coated her tongue. Grainy pieces swirled in the bottom. "I don't think it's good to be impulsive."

"Not all the time," Jonas agreed. "Little me was insane. I don't recommend that life." He took the mug from her and headed back inside. She followed him back to the dim kitchen where he dropped the mugs in the sink with a few other dishes. One pan looked like it held the remains of a bacon quiche, Craig's signature dish. Sasha had tasted it one time when a few teachers had come over to the Harper house for some kind of bash – Cinco de Mayo or Memorial Day. "But I'd like to see you loosen up."

"Well, I'd like to but–"

"Do something impulsive now."

Her eyes rounded. "What?"

He shrugged. "Dance. Move something. I don't know. It's your life. Just don't destroy anything." He grinned, looking first at her and then flitting his gaze around the room as though he were trying to guess what unexpected mischief she'd get up to.

She swallowed on a dry throat, looking anywhere but Jonas' face. Her mind was a blank. Impulsive, impulsive... When people talked about doing impulsive things, they talked about... what? Buying something? Kissing someone? She couldn't do that, for so many reasons. But there was one thing she wanted to fix.

Reaching out quickly, she turned down his shirt collar.

His laugh sounded rushed, as though he'd been holding his breath. She certainly had been.

"There, see? Feel better?" he asked when he collected himself.

She started to bite her lip but stopped herself.

"I don't know what I expected, but it makes sense that you'd do that."

Her eyebrows ticked lower. *Don't overanalyze.* "What would you do?" she challenged. The blood instantly left her cheeks after she heard her own words.

His answering look was brief, but it sent a shiver through her. He looked away. "Eh," he said, "it doesn't matter. I have tons of practice. It was nice hanging out with you today, though. Hope you have a good Christmas Break."

So that was it, then. The reality of the holiday slammed back into place. The suddenness of it hit her harder than she expected.

Did she really think that Jonas would spend the whole break with her? She'd slipped into a comfort that wasn't tenable. "Yes, yes," she said, moving to the door, embarrassed that he'd have to drive her back to the school. If they'd driven separately, she could make a clean exit. "You too."

When Sasha returned home that evening, Margot was sitting on the floor doing a puzzle. Well, *sitting* wasn't quite the right word. She was nearly doing the splits as she gracefully contemplated the unfinished work in front of her. According to the box, which tilted at an angle against her ankle, the picture should eventually be a fairy in front of a charming little door in a tree. Warm light showed the fairy's house within. At the moment, Margot had only succeeded in piecing together one free-standing transparent wing and two sides of the frame. Loose pieces jutted from the carpet, not even grouped by color.

Margot looked over her glasses when Sasha stepped in. Her fine features pinched into a smile, but she didn't rise. "I didn't think you'd be back so late," she said.

Sasha grunted, set her Star Wars travel mug, now long cold, on the counter, and pulled off her gloves. Snow clogged the streets now, and the drive from the school to the apartment had been harrowing enough that her shoulders slumped in relief.

"Did you do something after tearing down the set? Hopefully it didn't take *that* long." Margot pressed a brown, bark-looking piece against part of the frame and threw it away when it didn't fit. Folding her legs up under her, she straightened her spine and looked more pointedly at Sasha. Everything Margot did made her look like a dancer. And she was, when she wasn't working at the stationary store or the dog groomer. Her attitude matched someone who didn't work hard at all, but that wasn't the case with Margot. She flitted between each one of her jobs, putting in long hours, but seeming almost to arrive by accident, so it was easy to forget how hard she actually worked.

"We hung out afterwards," Sasha answered.

"We?"

"Jonas Harper. You know him." Sasha shrugged out of her coat to underline how nonchalant she was.

Margot's black bob fell over her shoulders in two dark sheets as she leaned forward. "The one you're madly in love with?"

"What?" Sasha's voice squeaked. She hated when it squeaked, unless it was on command to play Adelaide in *Guys and Dolls*. "Stop it!" Snow from her hair dripped onto the kitchen linoleum. She smudged the puddles around with her wet shoe, which only made it worse.

"I'm just teasing, Sasha," said Margot, standing amid the unkempt piles of puzzle pieces. Her shoulder sent one of their two Christmas stockings swaying back and forth on its hook on the mantle. The movement looked oddly forlorn.

Sasha chewed her lip. "I'm not... madly in love. We just had some cider. You know. To celebrate the break."

"The rules, I know." Margot rolled her eyes. "You've been dreading this break for weeks. Unless you're doing better now?"

Tears pricked at Sasha's eyes. She really was holding herself together splendidly. She cleared her throat. "Sure, yeah. Doing better." She eyed her friend. "Are you busy tomorrow?"

"Dogs and dance."

"Oh, right." The idea that other people could step in and do some of the official Christmas List items with her hadn't let go.

Cider with Jonas had been like a little adventure, one that made Christmas music sound more filled in with magic. "Well, maybe tonight we could watch *Psych*?"

"*Psych*?"

Sasha pursed her lips. "Fake psychic and his partner help the Santa Barbara police department solve–"

Her phone buzzed.

"–crimes. Has nobody heard of this show?"

She fished her phone out of her pocket. Margot stepped over the scattered puzzle pieces and grabbed a banana off the counter as Sasha put the phone to her ear. "Hello?"

"Hey, Sasha."

She hadn't checked the caller ID. Otherwise, she would have been prepared to hear Jonas' voice. "Hey." Her answering syllable came out supremely disinterested. Friend-like, maybe, but not excited.

"Hey. You made it home all right. Glad to see that. The roads up to Woodland Park are pretty slick."

"Yeah." *Why are you calling?* She didn't know what she was hoping for. The rules forbade getting any closer to him, but she couldn't deny how good it was to hear his voice, even after such a short time.

Margot perked up, sensing that Sasha's apparent lack of interest meant the opposite. Her roommate knew her well. Sasha waved her off.

"Do you want to send me that list you were talking about? I know the cider thing didn't really work out, but maybe I could do more of them with you. I was just thinking that I have time now, and my family doesn't have crazy elaborate plans, and it would be nice to help out a friend, do some fun things."

Sasha's stomach clenched in a pleasantly painful way. To stay *right here* would be heaven. Any response she gave would be the wrong one, but his offer was so kind and high-lighted the things she liked about him. Because, yes, she admitted to herself that she liked him. This was a thin line to walk.

Saying yes would mean she could see him again. But it also meant she would see him again. That could lead to nothing good. Her relationships always started like this – all happy butterflies until the guy moved on because she wasn't what he was looking for.

Saying no would mean she might not complete the List. At least she had Margot, when they both weren't working…

The rule was more important. It kept her safe from heart-break and the constant feeling that she wasn't enough. Without a relationship to emphasize it, she could push back those voices and stand more confidently on her own. Even if that meant she felt lonelier during the holidays.

"That's… that's really nice of you. Honestly. But it's a long list, and I don't think…"

Beside her, peeled banana in hand, Margot widened her eyes.

"Fifty-three items, right?" came Jonas' warm laugh.

"Fifty-six," she corrected. "You wouldn't want to do more of those."

"I would if you wanted to."

Sasha's shoe made a loud screech on the linoleum where she dragged it across the growing pool of water. "Sorry. That was–"

Jonas acted as if he didn't hear it. "No pressure. It's just a shame for people to be alone on Christmas."

"I'm not alone."

"Oh. Well. I just thought I'd offer, in case you wanted to. It's not…"

But he didn't finish. *Not what?* When he didn't complete his thought, she said, "That's okay. I appreciate the offer, but I'm perfectly fine here." She tapped her foot, sending up splashes, thinking of *Singin' in the Rain.*

"Okay. If you change your mind…"

The open-endedness of the offer ate at her. Why couldn't he

just say, "Well, screw you, then – we'll go back to being friends in January"? So much easier. She wouldn't have to keep that tab open in her mind. The option would disappear.

"I'm fine." She hung up the phone a millisecond before she realized how rude it was. Just like Jonas had described himself earlier. *Things just happened, and I'd realize it later.*

Margot took a thoughtful bite of banana. "Do you hate him?"

Sasha scoffed. "No. I don't hate him."

"Was that about the List?" Her roommate's voice was almost ethereal, like the fairy in the unfinished puzzle.

Sasha did have her phone volume turned up pretty loud. "Maybe. Yeah."

"Was he offering to do the List with you?"

"Yes." Her answer now was crisp, and she moved past Margot as she said it.

Her roommate pranced to keep up with her. "That's so sweet. How could you say no to that? You don't mind Jonas Harper, do you? He helped you build a dozen sets. Maybe you owe it to him."

Sasha halted. "I don't *owe* him anything," she said acidly.

"Oh, you know I didn't mean it that way!" Margot said innocently.

"We can do some of those things together instead."

"*Psych?*" The word on Margot's tongue was foreign.

"Yeah, if you want to." Sasha tried a smile. Something bleak was starting to settle again in her spirit, and she desperately wanted the feeling to fly off again.

"I'm busy tomorrow, but I could do that tonight. We could have a little TV marathon." Margot cuddled up to her, tangling her up in a sloth-like hug and resting her head on her shoulder. "But that's all I can do. I'm going to stay with my parents for a week starting day after tomorrow. I told you that."

Now that she mentioned it, she had, but Sasha had forgotten. She hadn't written in down in a list, and the end of the semester had been so busy... The bleak feeling, hard and cold, clung more relentlessly. Margot squeezed harder, a child's apology.

"You should do the rest of the List with Jonas," Margot whispered.

"The rule!" Sasha protested, though even the protest was an admission that the no-dating rule needed to be invoked at all.

"It's not dating, it's just… Christmas."

"But–"

"Is dating on your List?"

"No."

"Kissing?"

"No."

"Sex?"

"Margot!"

"Is it?"

"No."

"Then why not?" Margot twirled one of Sasha's curls around her finger. "Marie would be glad to know you still had a good Christmas."

Sasha sighed and stepped out of Margot's embrace. She was right about her sister. Marie always wanted the best for her. "You'll be gone until after Christmas?"

"I'm afraid so." Margot gave her another swift hug and then tapped the phone, still in Sasha's hand. "You should call him back."

RUDOLPH AND REVELATIONS

The best way to go about the List was to hit it like a blizzard, with as many items as possible at one time.

Sasha and Margot had managed to watch the "Christmas Joy" episode of *Psych*, an acceptable number of *Whose Line is It Anyway?* episodes to qualify, as well as the original cartoon version of "How the Grinch Stole Christmas," after Margot insisted that they weren't being Christmasy enough. At least both the roommates agreed that Christmas was the best time of year. Margot put up nutcracker figures and Halloween rats to stand for the Mouse King; Sasha put up her action figures of Han Solo, Princess Leia, and Luke Skywalker dressed in full Hoth gear with tauntauns amid her Christmas village. There was usually so much more, but, apart from their stockings and the little plastic tree they erected every year, there was almost nothing else in the apartment. Meager, by their standards.

Margot left on Monday, leaving her unfinished puzzle behind. Sasha cleaned it up and organized her fifty-six-item List into chunks that could be done at one time, to economize. That was how, on Monday evening, Jonas ended up in her apartment, sitting in front of the TV in fuzzy reindeer socks, surrounded by a flurry of paper clippings and a row of eggnog-filled shot glasses. Sasha eyed the holiday chaos fondly, as though it could protect her.

Setting down the pair of scissors and her half-finished snowflake, she leaned forward. On the TV, Santa, his perfectly round head gleaming, scolded Donner for having a deformed child. Sasha grabbed a shot glass. Though she hadn't added brandy to the eggnog, as she and Marie had before Marie had children, she still felt like this was a drinking game. "Shot!" she yelled, pitching back the mouthful of eggnog.

Jonas followed suit. "Why?"

"Santa just said something offensive." She'd chosen *Rudolph the Red-Nosed Reindeer* for two reasons: she hadn't seen it yet this year and it was the most unromantic movie left on the list.

"I haven't seen this since I was a kid," Jonas said, folding his piece of paper smaller. "Does that happen often?"

Sasha, wiggling her toes against her new soft socks, gestured theatrically to the row of shot glasses yet to be consumed.

"Geez…" He made a few more snips at the mangled white paper in his hand and gingerly unfolded it. A surprisingly intricate snowflake revealed itself. "Good?"

"Very good." The non-spiked eggnog somehow made her feel almost tipsy anyway.

Jonas held up a hand, numbering as he went. "Socks, Rudolph, snowflakes, eggnog. Are those all the ones we're doing today?"

"You want more?" Sasha teased, nudging his foot with hers and immediately regretting it.

"Well, it'll take a while to get through everything – although, this is a lot of…" He adjusted in the seat and held up the foot she had touched, waving it around as though it could speak for him. His expression was a mixture of amusement and disbelief, especially about the socks. Sasha had insisted on them. Either he would crumble under the weight of her Christmas List or he would help her get through every item. The challenge of it gave her a sort of new intensity.

"Not what you were expecting?"

He looked at her, as though responding to the challenge, and lifted his chin. The light in the dim apartment living room reflected off the sharp planes of his face and she realized again that they were alone.

She jumped up to grab some tape to stick the snowflakes to the walls. This was Warner's favorite list activity, after anything involving treats or presents. Jonas was at least a decent substitute.

"Can I see the List? Maybe there's something else we can do at the same time," he called out after her. It was hard to tell if he was serious.

She pointed at the screen. "Rudolph is about to be banned from reindeer games."

"Shot?" he suggested.

"Shot." She returned in time to put the snowflake on the wall behind the TV and shoot back another eggnog.

The politics of the couch felt complicated. It was a loveseat, two cushions. One side for her and one for him, but the cushions had worn in the middle so they tended to make people lean toward the center unless they held onto the armrests. Margot had a bad habit of sitting in the exact middle, on the line, whenever she wasn't watching TV with Sasha. The result was that Sasha had to *look* like she was avoiding Jonas in order to succeed at avoiding him. Jumping up periodically helped mitigate the problem.

"They really are mean to him," he mused, ripping off some tape and adding a couple more snowflakes to the wall. "Rudolph just has a shiny nose. That's not a bad thing, right?"

"But it's always the different kids that get picked on, no matter what." Realizing her comment had made things more serious than they needed to be, she began sweeping paper clippings into her hand. Jonas did the same.

"Yeah, kids can be mean," he agreed.

"I even did that when I was little. There was a boy in my class with really thick glasses and a bowl cut and I used to make fun of him all the time." She froze like a rabbit spotted by a snake. Or maybe a snake spotted by a hawk. *Stupid.* Why was she saying these incriminating things about herself? She wasn't proud of that. That wasn't the kind of person she was now. And here she was spilling some of the uglier parts of her as though the shots they drank were pure whiskey.

"Sounds like he looked a little silly–"

"He was really nice!" she lamented, crushing the pile of clippings in her fists and dropping back onto the sofa. "I wonder where he is sometimes, if he kept those glasses as an adult. I hope not. They looked ridiculous." She cut herself off again. Could she never say the right thing?

Jonas wore an amused smile. "You were young. It's okay. I've seen you with some kids who were stranger than that boy, and you are always nice to them."

"And I was bullied too," she went on, feeling the full confession forcing itself out of her. "I went to a mostly white school and so we'd get looks and people would say things. So I should have known better!" She gulped in a breath and grimaced. "There was a girl too, in fifth grade, that I used to tease because of her accent. I could only understand half of what she said. Her parents were Chinese. God, I was so mean." The tears she'd been holding back all week came horribly, undeniably pouring out. Miserable, she rose to put the paper in the trash and hide her face.

Sasha tried never to cry, because it was always loud. Even across the room, she doubted that Jonas could hear the TV over her sobs. Mortifying. And it made her cry more. The background noise stopped. Jonas must have paused the TV. She refused to turn around. She didn't want to see his sympathetic eyes or hear his questions. Better that he figure out a way to deal with this embarrassment for himself and leave her out of it.

When her tears finally subsided, she forced herself to turn around. Even if the rule forbid her to date Jonas, she still wanted him for a friend, and she probably blew her chance at either in one stocking-footed, eggnog drunk swoop. She was a bully. And a loud crier. How could he get beyond that?

She stared at the floor as she shuffled toward the loveseat, determined to hang onto the big armrest for dear life. That is, if Jonas stayed.

The TV clicked back on. Elves were singing. Santa was thoroughly unimpressed with their efforts and stormed out of the room.

Something cold touched the back of her arm. She looked up sharply. It was a shot glass.

"Shot," said Jonas.

She took it tentatively. They both drank more slowly than before, eyeing each other as if this were some western standoff. Her eyes had to be terribly bloodshot. One more embarrassment to add to the list. One more small way that she was no one's perfect woman.

They set down their glasses.

"I'm sorry," he said softly, and offered a hug. He didn't look particularly embarrassed or pitying or disgusted, or any of the things she expected to see on his face.

She regarded his open arms. Maybe it was weakness that made her fold into them. It wasn't a long hug, but it was strong and soothing and everything a hug should be.

They watched the rest of the movie in relative silence. Sasha spiked the rest of the eggnog shots. The two of them agreed wordlessly about the right times to drink. She didn't hang onto the arm of the loveseat, and neither did he.

The sweatshirt with the lace pattern simultaneously said "I don't care what you think" and "don't I look cute?" Yes, that seemed like the perfect balance.

Ever since Jonas left the night before, Sasha had felt warm with possibility. She could practically see the Rule – now an animate object like a notebook or something – glaring at her for forgetting herself. But she did her best to ignore it. Jonas hadn't been repulsed by her admission of bullying or her crying or her insistence that they both buy matching fuzzy socks. At the end of the evening, after Bumble put the star on the Claymation tree, he asked what was next.

What indeed?

Until the brandy wore off, they wrapped presents Sasha had gotten for Margot and a couple other friends. Amazingly, she didn't remember doing anything else that might embarrass her. She sang a little, but that was normal.

She twirled in front of the mirror. The sweatshirt didn't move as she did, but the angles confirmed that she looked good.

Maybe something could work with Jonas. She could like him without hating herself for it, at least. That had to be a good first step. Before he left her amidst a pile of ribbons and wrapping paper, they'd agreed to go skating.

Ice skating felt like a date. *Maybe it is!* She scolded herself. If this were really going to happen, it was better if she let things unfold naturally. Too bad there wasn't a montage song to speed up this part. Bing Crosby and Rosemary Clooney just needed to sing about snow and the train arrived in a different part of the country. That was the life she would love – one with all the tedious parts cut out. Plus, there was singing and vibrant dresses and dashing men who – with the exception of Rhett Butler – didn't blow off women because they had flaws.

After one last look, she swept out of the apartment. The car's soundtrack was *The Color Purple.* Not exactly Christmasy, but perfect for her range.

The rink was inside a shopping mall which, in retrospect, probably hadn't been the best choice. Ten full minutes of circling the parking lot finally led her to a space far enough away that she wished she'd brought an extra hat.

The air inside the mall smelled warm and plastic and recycled, like a water fountain. Huge golden ornaments hung suspended from the ceiling. A quick look at her phone told her she was five minutes late. Five minutes wasn't too much. Jonas wouldn't mind, not like her college boyfriend Franklin who had made any outing frosty and passive aggressive if she deigned to show up past the agreed time. It wasn't that she meant to be late. This time, the parking lot was full.

The rest of the way to the rink, she hustled, half-walking, half-running, gripping her coat around her.

He waited by the entrance, leaning against the plexiglass that separated the ticket counter from the rest of the mall. Large skates dangled from his hand. It was hard to tell from his posture if he was bored or upset.

She hurried up to him and opened her mouth to apologize.

"Miss Combs!" he greeted, his face lighting up.

She blew out a breath. "I'm so sorry! I didn't mean to be late."

A line formed between his brows. "Late?"

It wasn't a foreign word. "Yes, late."

"You weren't that late. Come on," he said. "Let's go."

She headed for the counter.

"I've got it." His hand hovered above her upper arm to usher her away but never actually made contact.

"I'll pay you back."

He waved dismissively. "It was eight dollars. I didn't know your shoe size, though."

"Seven."

The teenage clerk overheard and plopped a scuffed pair of white ice skates on the counter. She picked them up by the laces. Skates were always heavier than she remembered.

"Glad to see you made it here all right after all that brandy," she said. They passed a mini arcade area set back in an alcove and searched for the opening into the oval rink. The place was crawling with kids. They ran past, squealing. What looked like classes of fourth graders all dominated the ice. This wasn't going to be as romantic as her earlier fantasies had hoped.

"Yeah," he said, settling onto a bench occupied only by a diaper bag on one end. "I didn't realize how many problems there were with that movie!"

She exhaled. It would be all right. Shrugging out of her coat, she laced on the shoes. He didn't seem to notice her sweatshirt. It was a sweatshirt, so of course he didn't. Had she really started to think that he might be more than patient with her oddities, that he had actually started to like her? She chewed her lip and gave the laces an extra hard tug. Her ankles would never buckle, held in place as they were by that vice grip.

"There are a lot of kids here," she said ruefully.

"I teach fifth grade, Sasha," he replied, rising to his feet. "I don't mind kids."

"But it's Christmas Break."

He made a hissing sound and helped her up. Her cheap black gloves prevented her from actually touching him. She reminded herself that she'd be grateful for the gloves once they were out on the ice. Rarely did she fall, but she bobbed quite a bit and had to catch herself. Marie and her nieces thought she was a good skater, but that was only because the three of them were utterly hopeless, and Sasha could go backward.

Jonas and Sasha made it through the opening into the slippery rush.

"Is there a way this is supposed to be done? You know, with the List?" he said, raising his voice above the din of children and Tony Bennett.

She shook her head.

"Just showing up?"

"Check," she confirmed with a smile.

"Okay…" He glided beside her effortlessly, spinning around to face her and then skating beside her again. She was still bobbing, finding her feet. "I dated a skater in high school," he explained, giving his one-shouldered shrug.

She fought the urge to gnaw her bottom lip again. Instead, she made a noise that meant *Oh?*

"Yeah, she cheated on me with two different guys, so that didn't last long. Well, okay, it lasted all of junior year." He rolled his eyes and smiled, but there was something forced about it.

"Cheated on you?" The words burst out stronger than she meant to say them.

Jonas rolled up his sleeves to the elbows – it really was getting hot – and revealed his sunburst tattoo. "You'd be surprised how often that happens." His gaze drifted to the disco ball tucked amid the ceiling trusses, waiting to be lowered.

Besides one boy her sophomore year of high school who clearly had meant to ask a different girl to the dance, Sasha had never been cheated on, only broken up with. Repeatedly. "I can't believe anybody cheated on you," she said.

"Yeah, she wasn't the only one." He made a circle around her to lighten his words. She might be the superstar skater around Marie and the girls, but not Jonas, who might as well have practiced for national competitions. "Bad taste in women," he continued. "Some people obviously wouldn't cheat on their boyfriends." He gestured to her with his sunburst arm.

Her cheeks grew hot.

"Maybe I'm a typical guy, just looking for the most beautiful people, but they know they can play the field."

Now her cheeks burned for a different reason. Did he not think she was beautiful?

When she snapped out of her momentary rage, he was looking straight at her with a wicked, teasing smile. She hit him.

The movement sent her skates sliding wildly along the ice. Her legs shot out from under her but she caught herself backward on her gloved hands, looking completely foolish, like a deflated crab. Two pre-pubescent boys skated by, sniggering into their hands.

Jonas laughed and hauled her back to her feet. No more talk of exes after that. The performance on Friday and breakfast food choices and an annoying song that kept playing on the radio took up the next hour. Sasha gave him ideas about what to buy his brother Will for Christmas. She'd only met him once, but he had clearly liked *Assassin's Creed*, and a new version of the game had come out that year, so that gift idea won.

During their conversation, Jonas kept trying to keep her from falling again. Part of her was irritated that he didn't seem to think she could keep upright without him, but another part was horribly pleased that he kept touching her – all innocent touches to her arm or upper back. By the end of the skate, she was tempted to wobble more often just to see what he would do. Maybe he wasn't interested in her the way she was in him, but if that were true, then why was he spending so much time with her? Why was he completing her Christmas List? And why did he look for an excuse to touch her?

Unpleasantly sweaty but otherwise happy, Sasha toddled her way off the ice. She and Jonas unlaced their skates and handed them back to the unenthusiastic attendant, and headed out to her car. ("It might be icy," Jonas said.)

It was still piercingly cold outside, but her body heat inside the jacket kept her warm. The two of them didn't talk, since the icy breeze would just rip their words away.

At the car, she unlocked the door but then turned, her back to the driver's side. Under layers of jacket and sweatshirt, her heart thudded. Somewhere in her mind, an alarm was screaming. *The rule! The rule!* But they had drunk hot cider, watched Rudolph, worn matching socks, had brandy-spiked eggnog shots, made paper snowflakes, and skated together. And he had touched her. All that had to mean something.

She looked up at him. As he blinked against the wind, his gaze was a little uncertain. His five o' clock shadow had become more pronounced since he hadn't had to shave for work. Again, the collar of his jacket was a little askew. She resisted the urge to fix it again. But the movement would have been too forward, too intimate. If he wanted to be with her, then she wouldn't resist, but she didn't want to force him into an uncomfortable position by making her feelings too obvious. So she paused a moment to give him an opening, halfheartedly fiddling through her purse with one hand.

He stood rather close to her, but that could have been because of a patch of black ice near his feet. His cheeks were pink. Maybe the cold wind. It truly was freezing. She couldn't stand in limbo for much longer without losing feeling in her face.

Then he leaned forward. She drew in a breath and braced herself. This was it! Did she want this? Yes. The alarm didn't matter then. Jonas knew her better than the others. She tilted her head up to meet his. This could actually turn into a happy ending…

She closed her eyes. Her lips met stubble.

The door behind her opened and a breath of cold air swept across her, as though it had come from the car. She opened her eyes to find that Jonas had stepped back, a note of horror in his expression.

"I'm so sorry," he exclaimed. "I didn't mean…" He gave an awkward laugh.

Dread coursed through her, thick as syrup. He hadn't meant to kiss her after all. And she had closed her eyes and leaned in while he simply meant to open her car door.

She had to get home. Now. And curl up into a ball of shame.

For a moment, she couldn't speak. Jonas, now two feet away, might as well have been ten thousand miles. This was the kind of thing that friends couldn't recover from. She had kissed his cheek!

Every thought made her want to burrow deeper into the ground and never come out.

"I'm sorry," he said again. His smile came fairly easy but she knew him well enough to see that he felt uncomfortable.

"Okay," she breathed. "No, I…" But she had no idea what she was saying. In a flash, she disappeared into the car, closing the door shut between them.

AFTERMATH

When Debbie Reynolds and Gene Kelly sang about having a good morning, it was anything but.

On the couch, Sasha wrapped her blanket closer around her, pulling it up to her neck. In front of the couch where she lay were a couple paper snowflakes and open Blu-ray disks. The room smelled faintly of old popcorn. Morning light streamed harshly through the blinds, making the outline of the tauntaun glow white from its place on the mantle.

She groaned. In a flurry of emotion that she knew from painful experience never led anywhere good, she had all but kissed Jonas in the mall parking lot. A curse threatened to rise in her throat. How could she have been so shortsighted? Jonas was helping her through the List – he was trying to make her Christmas better. And what did she do?

She pressed a hand to her forehead. Even as she was doing it, she knew it was dramatic, but Margot wasn't here to see and call her out on it. She could be as dramatic as she liked, so she took full advantage.

Even the impeccable dancing on the washed-out screen didn't lift her spirits like usual. Like the Christmas songs, the joy of the musical had been hollowed out. A puff without cream. And what use was that?

Her phone buzzed. She took it out from where she'd been cradling it against her stomach, checking every half hour or so to see if Jonas would call off their friendship. Her mind felt alert and fuzzy at the same time.

The caller ID said it was a video call from Marie. Sasha sniffed and sat up, wiping her eyes. She'd forgotten all about their planned call. Her hair was a messy nest from being on the couch and her eyes felt puffy. Marie would see right through her. The phone buzzed again, insistent. "Fine," she muttered to it as she paused the movie and allowed the call through.

Marie's face appeared, impeccable and awake. In the background was a white wall. Sasha counted the time zones between Colorado and Germany. It was almost dinnertime there.

"My gosh!" Marie exclaimed. "Are you all right, Sasha?"

"Hello to you too."

"Are you okay?"

"No. My break is ruined." The drama she'd vowed to indulge came barreling through in her tone. She hadn't expected to speak to anyone today.

"Tell me."

Sasha did. The story didn't take long, even with hedging and sniffling. "At least Christmas is the day after tomorrow," she finished. "It'll be better when it's over."

"You can't say that! We can still do something on our List together." Marie held up a manicured nail, painted plum. She never did her nails unless for a special occasion.

"Your nails look nice," Sasha began.

"Hush. Listen." Thready music began in the background. Sasha turned up the phone's volume. It was "Silent Night" by the Temptations. "'Twas the night before Christmas," Marie quoted, in a voice that sounded more like a bad impression of the pickle from Veggie Tales than the member of the band.

Despite herself, Sasha huffed out a laugh, then hummed along to the singing part. No need to tell her that she'd already crossed off this item. Singing with her sister was the best.

"Is that the best you can do?" Marie asked.

"At the moment, yes." Her voice would crack if she tried it in the regular way.

The intro ended and Marie stopped the song. She leaned toward the screen and raised her eyebrows. "See? Check one item off. You'll be okay, Sasha."

Sasha swallowed. "Are the girls there?"

"You can't get off that easily," Marie protested, but she left the iPad on the counter and disappeared to get Warner and Emma. Their little faces peered into the screen. "Auntie Sasha's going to the craft fair tomorrow!" Marie told them somewhere off to the side.

Sasha's mouth opened to protest, but no words came out. She would probably still go. The Combs Christmas instinct ran deep.

"The craft fair!" Emma shrieked.

"Remember, we went to the market earlier," Marie reminded them.

"I want to go to the craft fair." Warner looked expectantly at Sasha as though she could wave a magic wand like Cinderella's godmother and make it happen.

Sasha shrugged one shoulder, then the other one so they matched and didn't remind her of a certain someone. Her almost-kiss, besides making her insides feel hot and twisted whenever she thought of it, could also have doomed her musical productions for future years. Who else would step up and help her so much with the sets? *Someone will. You're catastrophizing.* It was a word Marie had taught her for when Sasha started spiraling.

Incoming call, the dropdown box announced.

Jonas.

"Uh, I'll call you back," Sasha sputtered. "Bye. Bye, girls. I'll get you something nice at the craft fair. Your mama too. Bye."

She raised the phone to her ear. "Hello?" As soon as the word escaped her lips, it sounded desperate, breathless.

"Hey, Sasha." Jonas, by comparison, sounded cool as ice.

She gripped the blanket covered in popcorn crumbs. Good thing he couldn't see her right now. "Hi."

"Hey, I just wanted to apologize if that was weird yesterday. I don't know what that was. I…"

She jumped in. "Oh, no, it's fine."

"I didn't…" He faded away again, then blew out a breath.

Her skin burned hot. This conversation was just peachy so far. Biting her lip to keep from saying anything else, she cast a mournful look at the frozen trio on the screen and felt their commiseration.

"I…" He cleared his throat. "I'd still like to do some of the things on your List if you're up for it. If you're not too…"

"Too what?" Would the man never finish his sentences? This one seemed particularly important.

"If we're still good." There was the tiniest hint of defeat in his tone, as though *he* had tried something with *her* instead of the other way around, and was seriously regretting it. Could that be true? The idea bolstered her

She allowed the tiniest hint of her feelings to bleed through her voice as well. "Yeah, we're still good." After a held breath, she added, "Did you… Were you really trying something in the parking lot? I mean, I know I'm dazzling, but…"

Silence on the other end.

Possible responses cut through the loud white noise crackling in her head: *It's okay that you tried to kiss me.* *"I'm just kidding – never believe anything I say." "I know you wouldn't do that." "Do you want to come over and watch* Singin' in the Rain *with me?" "You know, I really like you, Jonas."* None of them came out of her mouth.

Finally, a feeble laugh. "I'm glad we're good," he said. "Just let me know what's next on the list. I'm seeing my family on Christmas Eve for most of the day, and I should go shopping for presents at some point, I guess, but I'm free other than that."

He dodged the question! Frustration surged through her before subsiding, replaced with disbelief. People only dodged questions they didn't want to answer. *No, I didn't try to kiss you* would have been simple. Confusion tinged with optimism replaced her irritation.

"I've got chestnuts," he added.

"Excuse me?"

"One of my students gave them to me for Christmas. They're in a jar and look nasty, but I thought roasting chestnuts was maybe on your List."

A smile quirked Sasha's mouth. "It isn't."

"Oh."

"But you can bring them over anyway," she amended. "I do have a gas stove."

When Jonas looked at his jar of chestnuts, he had thought of her. He acted flustered about the events at the mall. He didn't answer her question. Maybe, despite everything, he did like her after all.

CHESTNUTS ROASTING ON AN OPEN FIRE

It was December 23, and Jonas came over to roast chestnuts over a (very small) fire. He stood at her shoulder, huddled by the little gas stove with a chestnut balanced on a toothpick. It was the most ill-conceived idea ever invented by grown adults. Sasha's fingers felt hot near the blue flame of the burner.

He turned to her. "This is not working."

"Not at all."

They brandished the pale chestnuts and set them on the counter.

"You probably won't add that to the List, then," Jonas said, smiling.

She tipped her mouth down. "Mmm, maybe not."

The careful flirting she'd been doing felt an awful lot like their normal friendship. Maybe she acted this way with Margot too. There was no telling. She'd have to be more obvious if he was going to catch on, but that felt dangerous. She *thought* he might like her, yet he was a patient guy who would go through a lot of crying and confessions and awkward missed kisses to keep a friendship. If only she could be sure!

"Ornaments are a must, though," she went on as they moved toward the loveseat where she'd set up the materials they needed. "We need to bring them to the Christmas Eve craft fair tomorrow."

"Oh, right! You mentioned that one."

She laid a hand over her heart. "It's the most important one."

Dimples appeared as he surveyed her neatly piled craft supplies. His high cheekbones looked artlessly beautiful when he made that face. She wanted to study it. "Always the teacher," he said, almost catching her looking at him.

She stared down at the wooden circles and ribbons, portioned off into sections in preparation for his arrival. "Aren't you? You have that Mr. Harper voice."

He squared up to her, picking up a wood slice absently with one hand. "I don't use my Mr. Harper voice on you."

"Yes, you do."

"When have I done that?"

"Just now. When you asked that question."

His eyebrows lowered. Then he chuckled. "That was only kind of my Mr. Harper voice. The real thing is frightening. Really gets the kids in line." He fixed his expression into mock seriousness.

"Why don't you show me?" Something about the challenge sent her stomach into knots.

His expression softened with surprise before he caught himself and played along. He pointed past her at an imaginary student. "You, Mary Beth, you need to sit down. Recess is *over!*" His imperious command was nothing like the voice she'd heard him use around real students.

Dutifully, she sat. He sat next to her, still twirling the slice of wood in his fingers instead of getting to work. Was he waiting for something? Was he waiting for her?

He had to like her. He had to. All the evidence pointed to it.

Every performance she'd seen had taught her to recognize the signs, and they were blinking in her face. He liked her.

Her ribcage felt tight with anticipation. He stole a look at her, almost sheepish, his dark eyes bright. If he kissed her now…

If he kissed her now, everything would be different. They could never go back to being just friends. Eventually they would break up because she couldn't hold his interest. She found it hard to breathe. The air around them thinned and longing filled her up where air should be.

All the songs she grew up singing rushed back to her. It was Christmas Eve eve, and magic sparkled in the air. She wouldn't be Sasha the Catastrophizer – she would be Sasha the Bold, Sasha of Second Chances, Sasha who wanted to love the man in front of her.

Do something impulsive now.

He opened his mouth. Maybe it was to speak, but before he could get out a sound, her lips were on his. She wrapped numb hands around him. The front of his shirt was still warm from the stovetop. Even through the kiss, her mind wouldn't stop. A million voices stood at the gate, speaking at once, but for now they were muted. She was Sasha the Brave, the one kissing Jonas Harper.

At first he stiffened – with surprise, she guessed – but then he relaxed and joined her. Feeling began to return to her hands when he kissed her back, gentle but persistent. She was right! Jonas, the man who could woo any girl, chose her. Emotion flooded through her. Relief – relief that someone so wonderful, who had seen so many of her ugly moments, could still want her.

CHRISTMAS EVE CRAFT FAIR

Sasha wore a red dress and black heels to the craft fair on Christmas Eve. She might not have brought ornaments for the first time ever (kissing left little time for making them,) but she did bring herself.

The smell of hot cider wafted through the warehouse of wooden beams and exposed brick. Who knows where they had managed to find some cider in this town? Maybe they'd bought it all for this event before she and Jonas went looking for their own. Tables crowded the edges of the space as though they were covered by one long, continuous, multi-colored tablecloth, leaving the center clear for dancing. Her feet tingled. It wasn't that she was a great dancer, but others would say she was adequate. She'd played many a chorus part in school that involved some dancing.

Guests were just starting to arrive and browse the craft tables. Her gauzy cocktail dress made her the fanciest person in the room. Today, though, she didn't care that she stood out. Today she was still Sasha the Bold from the day before. Red fit her mood.

Scanning the space, she lighted on her grandmother, a short

but rigid figure in the shadows behind one of the booths. Sasha clipped toward her.

"Grandma!"

She took Sasha's face in two dry hands and kissed her cheeks. "Merry Christmas, Sasha girl!"

"Merry Christmas."

"Do you have the ornaments?" Grandma's dark eyes scrutinized Sasha's hands, empty but for a small purse. Her crow's feet deepened when she didn't see what she was looking for.

Sasha beamed. "No. Sorry."

Grandma raised an admonishing finger. Though she stood only up to Sasha's nose, she had the fierceness of a hawk. "But you always have them. You and Marie always bring them."

The table did look a little sparce without them. Grandma always made different things each year, a rotation of crafts she'd worked on in the months leading up to the event. Crocheted drink coasters, repackaged teas, layered paper gift tags, and knitted head scarves were the offerings this time. A few pinecones artfully held the spot where all the missing ornaments were supposed to go.

"I'm sorry," Sasha repeated, her face matching her words now. "Marie's not here this year."

Grandma pursed her lips knowingly. She grunted. "And you're running off with a man now?"

She looked behind her in case Jonas had arrived. Nothing, although more people were lining up to get in. It was barely seven o' clock, so he still had time. She couldn't wait to dance with him and see which tables he liked and hear how Will liked his present.

"You look very nice," Grandma explained.

"I always look nice," Sasha protested, frowning.

"But you look *very* nice."

She couldn't deny it. The view in the mirror had made her smile before tripping out of the apartment.

"Who is he? Is he treating you right?"

"Yes, yes," she replied, impatient. Now that her mind had turned back to Jonas, she wanted to go searching for him.

"Sasha!" Grandma snapped.

She returned her attention to the severe woman behind the table.

"Your mind is fluff, Sasha girl." Grandma's scowl melted into a reluctant smile. "Go on and have some peppermint bark."

Sasha's eyes widened. She hadn't seen that treat when she came in. But then, she'd been distracted.

"I know it's your favorite." Grandma shooed her away.

Maybe it wouldn't be so terrible coming to the craft fair without Marie. She would tell her and the girls all about it in the morning, and, in the meantime, she could eat peppermint bark and dance with Jonas. That wasn't bad at all. She smiled around a piece of white chocolate. Crunchy candy canes coated the top. So good!

Behind her, the brass band adjusted in their seats. The gallery lighting gleamed off the instruments, casting sparkles around the room.

7:15. Where was Jonas?

He did say he planned to spend the day in Woodland Park with family. The roads were a little slick, so he was probably on his way. Besides, the entrance to the warehouse wasn't easy to find the first time. He'd be here.

"I didn't want to make a bad choice." His words from yesterday returned to her. They'd both lounged diagonally on the loveseat, his arms around her middle. As he said it, he'd gestured with one hand and she touched his sunburst tattoo. The memory of it felt comfortable and thrilling all at once.

"Bad choice?" she'd murmured.

"That's why I didn't kiss you."

"But you're glad I did, right?"

A tiny twist in her stomach sent her looking at the door again.

He promised he'd be here, and Jonas was reliable. He came to build junior high musical sets day after day even though it wasn't in his job description. He continued to help her strike items off her Christmas List after she'd cried. He would come.

Popping the last of the peppermint bark into her mouth, she flipped open the clutch purse and checked her phone. No texts.

Texting and driving wasn't safe. Of course there were no texts from him. He was a responsible person.

The band struck up "A Marshmallow World," clear and loud and ringing. She exhaled. She'd give him until 7:30, and then she'd call.

As the fair filled up, the high-ceilinged room grew hot. Murmured voices became more insistent. Laughter burst out more loudly. Glasses clinked and the white lights strung high along the walls glowed brightly. Even without her ornaments, a perfect craft fair for Christmas Eve.

Except that there was no Jonas.

What had he said next? Had he said anything? He hadn't seemed bothered by her initiative yesterday – in fact, he'd emphatically kissed her back – but was he having second thoughts now? She hadn't asked him if he wanted her to kiss him. Maybe that violated the rules of consent… *Don't catastrophize. He gave you plenty of signs, and he clearly liked it, so calm down!* Her inner teacher could only dampen the panic starting to rise in her throat.

7:30.

She drew out her phone and stepped into the cool hallway, away from the brunt of the noise.

Ring… ring… ring…

She tapped one foot and drew her free hand over the coats packed into the rack across from the exterior door. Fur coat, nylon coat…

Ring… ring…

Wool coat.

Ring… "You have reached the voicemail box of Jonas Harper."

She hung up. He wasn't answering his phone. What did this mean?

He was in danger, or hurt. His address wasn't hard to find – she remembered it, anyway. She could leave right now and rescue him. She glanced at the glass-paneled door. If the problem were serious, though, would the family want her there? If it wasn't serious, wouldn't he have texted to let her know he wasn't coming? Her muscles stiffened with indecision.

To silence her thoughts, she moved back into the craft fair. The music and the food and the people drowned her. But just for a moment. Marie's absence pierced her as though she'd just learned her sister wouldn't be there, at the most important holiday event of the year.

The lump in her throat wouldn't let her swallow. Even the bright brass band and families dancing in the warm light started to take on that hollow quality.

The next hour was checking the door, checking her phone, and helping Grandma behind the table. She did have a cup of cider – decidedly not powdered – and danced two songs. Jonas couldn't determine everything about her Christmas. When she still hadn't heard anything from him at 8:30, a new kind of dread filled her. What if he was dead?

Grandma tried to swat down Sasha's swirling blizzard of emotions to no avail.

At 9:30, she left. No word from Jonas the entire night. Either he had forgotten about her, didn't want to see her, or was dead in a ditch somewhere. None of those options made her feel any better about walking out into the icy parking lot in heels, alone in the dark. Cars still filled most of the spots. She could hear the party from out here. It would go until at least 11:00, but she couldn't enjoy it anymore. Worry and anger and sadness had ruined it.

Jonas had seen new, unflattering sides of her this week.

Maybe he didn't want her to kiss him. He'd just played along because everyone liked being kissed. Now that he had some time away, he must have come to his senses, realized that their friendship would never be the same, and decided to cut off all communication then and there. Maybe it was better that way, but the fiery part of her fumed that he would ghost her like that.

She slumped into the driver's seat. With the door still open, she removed her black stilettos and replaced them with fluffy driving shoes. Before she'd left that evening, she'd made a list, of course. It included bringing sensible shoes to drive in, a coat that matched her stunning dress, and the items she would pack into the tiny silver clutch. A single tissue was folded neatly inside. She slammed the car door and took it out. The tissue was meant to fix her eyeliner if it got too hot, or help if she got a whiff of cinnamon and had to sneeze.

In the dark parking lot, sitting in her car alone, she thought she should have packed more of them.

MIDNIGHT

The instrumental chorus of "Defying Gravity" played somewhere. Consciousness swam back into focus and Sasha peeled open her scratchy eyes. What time was it?

She groped for her phone, which played the tune again – her ringtone. The artificial glow made the only light in the room.

Jonas Harper.

She shot up in bed and struck the answer button. "Hello?" she slurred.

"Sasha! I didn't know if you'd still be awake." He didn't sound dead, but he hadn't come to the Christmas Eve craft fair. Sleep still clung to her, and details fuzzed over in the black room.

She held the phone far enough away to read the time. Close to midnight.

"Are you home?" he asked. "Let me start again. I'm so sorry I didn't come to the Christmas Eve thing. I, well… Are you home?"

"I'm home." Nothing he said made sense. She flicked on the bedside lamp and adjusted the head wrap she'd bought from Grandma's craft table.

"I want to explain. I'm so sorry. Could I come over?"

At midnight? She squinted down at her Scooby Doo pajamas. "What happened?"

"I'm… I'm actually here."

"Here?" Grabbing her robe and turning on lights, she stumbled from the room. "Are you okay?" She'd laid out the presents from Marie, Grandma, and Margot on the floor so she'd have something pleasant to wake up to. There was no room for self-pity on Christmas, she had told herself last night as she washed her face too vigorously.

"I'm fine. I'm okay," he confirmed. "If you don't want me to…"

She yanked the door open. Jonas wore a black coat over a dark red button-down shirt with a black tie and slacks. The collar was askew on the left side. His pant legs were wet from the knee down. One had a rip, its mangy look matching his wild, wet hair. Redness colored his high cheekbones. Only one hand wore a glove. In that hand, he held his cell phone. The bare hand punched something on the screen. He paused awkwardly when she opened the door.

"What happened to you?"

"I'll show you," he said.

"You look freezing." She moved away so he could come in if he wanted to. With his first step forward, self-consciousness set in. She was in a robe and pj's while he stood there in a shirt and tie. Embarrassment turned rapidly into anger. Earlier that night, she had been beautiful, expecting him to join her for the most important night of the holidays, to fill the void left by her sister. And instead he showed up late at night on Christmas Eve, at her house, and hadn't even offered an explanation. At least Santa brought presents.

She slammed the door behind him. "Where were you? I waited for you."

He was still fiddling with his phone, not looking at her.

"Jonas!" Her own stern but reasonable teacher voice had given way to her grandmother's voice, and that was much less forgiving. "This is important. Pay attention to me."

"Here." He shoved the phone in her hand and took a step back.

The screen showed pictures of a nighttime road lit like a crime scene. Four cars stopped at odd angles in front of a barrier of snow. One of them was Jonas' black Civic. Two others crunched together, front bumper folded into a Subaru hatchback.

"The road was blocked and there was an accident."

Pressing her lips together, she gripped the phone that held the answer to the riddle that had plagued her all night. "You still could have called."

"It's a dead spot."

"How convenient."

"No, really! I stayed to clear the road and make sure everybody was okay."

The hurt still wouldn't go away. "Why didn't you go back up the road for a second to let me know what was going on?"

For a second, he looked gobsmacked. "I didn't think of it."

"You didn't think of it!" The repetition came out as one scoffed word. The trouble was that she wanted to believe him – she did believe him – but was that enough? He'd abandoned her when she needed him most, not only to validate what had happened between them, but to help her through her first Christmas alone.

"Sasha." Jonas reached toward her.

She gave him his phone back. He looked mildly surprised, as though it didn't belong to him. "Maybe this is a sign," she said, knowing how she sounded as she was saying it. "Maybe we're not meant to be more than friends. I'm sorry I jeopardized everything." She felt heat at the corners of her eyes. Sniffing, she added, "I'm glad you're okay. Your car's okay?"

His mouth softened. It wasn't a smile exactly, but that's what it wanted to be. "Yeah, car's okay."

In the ensuing pause, he cleared his throat.

"Water?" she offered, gesturing toward the obvious kitchen to their right. He didn't move. What was she supposed to do with him now? They could still be friends, but any more talk could wait until the morning. Her mouth worked around the words that would ask him to leave. They just wouldn't come out.

"I wanted to dance with you," he said suddenly. His voice sounded scratchier, as though water really would help. "I was looking forward to it. I wanted to go to the party and..."

"I wore a red dress." She said it like a point in an argument.

Her comment didn't throw him. He only nodded. "I bet. I bet it looked good."

"And they played music."

"How did your grandmother feel about having no ornaments?"

"Peeved," she said delicately. Her muscles started to relax.

Backlit by the kitchen light, he breathed, almost a sigh. "I tried to call. I really did." He shifted his weight. "We don't need to let this influence things at school. We can still hang out like before and not let things get weird."

Heaviness settled in her stomach. "Is that what you want?"

"That's what you want, isn't it?" His brows fell in a serious line. All his attention was pinned on her and she nearly faltered under the question. Either answer was damning.

She couldn't deny what she felt, but she had to give him a way out if he wanted it. "I don't know," she answered slowly.

His eyes fell. "Here's the honest truth." The line of his shoulders looked unnatural and stiff. "I can't stop thinking about you. The more we spend time together, I just think about you all the time. And I was hoping that you might want something more, but..."

He took another breath, and Sasha found she was holding hers.

"I totally understand if you don't want that. You know, it's easy to get caught up in the moment, but it's probably not a good idea since we work together…"

Now he was rambling.

"I thought you decided you didn't want this." She indicated all of her Scooby-Doo-clad self.

"I wouldn't ghost you!"

"That's what I thought!" When had she started smiling?

He pulled off his other glove and stuffed it in his jacket pocket. "So you do want to give this a try, then?"

"Obviously. I opened the door for you at midnight after you left me at a party."

"And you kissed me," he pointed out teasingly, not moving any closer.

"And you? You're not… bothered?" She looked away. All her little failures stung like bees.

"Bothered?" His cold hand took hers. "I showed up here. I feel like that counts for something. If you want me, then I want you."

When she looked up, his eyes were alive. "I do want you."

Eyebrows raised, he slowly lowered his head, tentative, as though they hadn't kissed before. She waited, filled with giddiness and longing all at once.

Without warning, he pulled back. "I thought you were mad at me."

"I was mad at you." She closed some of the distance to coax him to come closer.

He planted a soft kiss on her lips. Somehow it was even sweeter since she was in her pajamas and head wrap, with no makeup on. Their first kiss had been a test of her bravery, her willingness to overthrow the relationship rule. This kiss meant that he liked her too. Both kisses deserved to be in some hall of fame.

"Sasha Combs," he said, soft in her ear. His baritone voice sent shivers down her spine. "I want to dance with you, and watch *Whose Line*, and roast those stupid chestnuts."

"They were terrible," she laughed.

He backed up, holding her loosely around the hips. "Almost as bad as Marcus Amilcar's cupcakes. Do you remember those?"

Salt instead of sugar. "Ugh, yes! At the cast party?" Multiple students had eaten cupcakes and complained loudly about them before she'd identified the problem. Jonas had discreetly gotten rid of the tray while she explained Marcus' mistake to him. "Wait, you ate one of the chestnuts?"

He placed a hand on his stomach. "Of course. I had to try them."

"You're nasty."

"And you're a drama queen."

A fierce, lopsided smile twisted her lips. "Pushover."

"Party pooper."

"Hey, I was wearing a red dress! And you never showed."

"I showed up *late*," he corrected.

Their voices had gotten lower and their faces closer again as they spoke.

"So, we're doing this?" His lips hovered a breath above hers.

"I think you may be my boyfriend, Mr. Harper." She couldn't keep the smile out of her voice. Then, more seriously, "Thank you for being here for me. This Christmas would have been nothing without you."

He squeezed her tighter. "Any time, Sasha. Any time."

The glowing light behind them wasn't twinkle lights, but the kitchen, and she didn't stand in a red dress and heels, but Scooby Doo pajamas and a robe. She did stand with Jonas Harper, though, her best friend.

Right about now, Warner and Emma would be waking up Marie on Christmas morning in Germany.

Despite everything, for all of them, it was a magical Christmas after all.

JUST FOR FUN

Search the name of each story and you'll find Christmasy playlists for them on Spotify!

If you want more Short & Sweet Christmas Romances, be sure to join the email list to get alerted when a new title comes out! Simply go to this link: bit.ly/anneharrisonnewsletter.

www.ingramcontent.com/pod-product-compliance
Lightning Source LLC
Chambersburg PA
CBHW021146190726
48288CB00008B/2853